LONGLISTED FOR THE ASPEN WORDS LITERARY PRIZE

LONGLISTED FOR THE ANDREW CARNEGIE MEDAL

"[*The Graybar Hotel* is] well-written and worth reading for Dawkins's craft and insight, but it's also an occasion to consider an industry that has little to do with rehabilitation, and that makes it nearly impossible for its participants to recuperate their lives. . . . Almost every [story] reflects with devastating compassion on the guilt and regrets of the criminals inside."

—*Chicago Tribune*

"Dawkins is a wickedly skilled storyteller. . . . Despite its subject matter, *The Graybar Hotel* is finally uplifting. . . . toughly courageous, unflinching, and unapologetic."

—*O, The Oprah Magazine*

"[Dawkins's] prison stories are insightful and well written, and they ring true. Dawkins possesses the acquired wisdom of a man who's been there, done that and, unfortunately, is staying there."

—*Houston Chronicle*

"The best book of short stories by an MFA grad imprisoned for life you'll read this year—or probably ever."

—*New York*

"[A] book that is remarkable for its modesty, realism, and humanity. . . . Dawkins has a genius for bringing characters to life and making mundane situations compelling, if only because they feel so real. . . . [Dawkins] has produced a book that is not only moving and genuine, but genuinely important; one that, without resorting to shock tactics, powerfully conveys the perverse inhumanity of mass incarceration."

—*The Guardian*

"Dawkins can write. His prose skillfully carries the reader directly into the setting of all of his stories: the jailhouse or prison. He captures this unnatural and uniquely terrible world with precision and clarity. Most readers haven't spent time incarcerated; all will come away from this superb collection feeling as if they have."

—*New York Journal of Books*

"Dawkins brings us real news and art, employing strange conceits—inmates collect-calling strangers, or preparing for an intramural softball game, or acquiring the ability to disappear—to expose prison's most powerful weapon against minds and bodies: not violence, but boredom."

—*Vulture*

"Reading *The Graybar Hotel* is as close as most people would ever want to get to going to prison. Dawkins's characters are as indelible as the prison tattoos he describes with wry precision, from Depakote Mo to Doo-Wop to Jonnie Rae. The clichés about prison life—cigarettes as currency, strained race relations, a lot of television watching, and occasional violence—are deftly skirted here as Dawkins plays with the claustrophobia of his characters' condition by moving in and out of their lives before and during incarceration. Dawkins, who is serving life without parole for murder, is a formidable new talent."

—*LitHub*

"This short story collection explores the life of prisoners with both intoxicating and unparalleled insight and surprising humor."

—*Time Out*

"[A] powerful collection of stories about how inmates survive and struggle in prison."

—*San Diego Magazine*

"A Western Michigan University MFA graduate serving life for a drug-fueled 2004 Kalamazoo murder, Dawkins chronicles the occasionally colorful, often despondent, and mostly tedious lives of contemporary inmates. . . . Dawkins writes empathetic, thoughtful pieces about those who long for the outside."

—*Shelf Awareness*

"A well-turned and surprising addition to prison literature."

—*Kirkus Reviews* (starred review)

"What's freshest and most surprising here is Dawkins's absolute focus on the humanity of those behind bars—of how inmates survive, or don't, as they struggle to maintain self and sanity in the face of the tedium, deprivation, and loneliness of incarceration. A fully realized debut."

—*Library Journal* (starred review)

"In stories that range from high-definition realism to wistful surrealism, Dawkins illuminates the nuances of prison life from the fragility of inmate friendships to the constant assault of memories and regrets, sensual deprivation, the intricate web of lies and power plays, and the many shades of stoicism. Sorrowful, hard-hitting, and compassionate, these finely formed, quietly devastating stories are told with unusual and magnetizing authority."

—*Booklist* (starred review)

"Dawkins's tales impress with the authenticity of real-life experience, and his prose is rich in metaphor and imagery. . . . His often wryly amusing observations about the routines of prison life make him a striking guide for navigating the terrain."

—*Publishers Weekly*

"In *The Graybar Hotel*, Curtis Dawkins brings the contemporary short story at its best into the shadowy world of America at its worst, behind the bars of its overpopulated and ubiquitous prisons. These brilliantly crafted stories—with their formal inventiveness, savory dialogue, meticulous detail, and succinctly compassionate portraiture—are as much a manual in how to write original short fiction as in how to think about prisons. Still, anyone who wants to understand America's correctional system through the clarifying lens of great fiction will now have to know three indispensable books: Malcolm Braly's *On the Yard*, for the social novel; Chester Himes's *Yesterday Will Make You Cry*, for the bildungsroman;

and now Curtis Dawkins's *The Graybar Hotel*, for the short story."

—Jaimy Gordon, author of the National Book Award–winning novel *Lord of Misrule*

"Curtis Dawkins draws from his direct experience to paint a picture of jailhouse life in all its grimness. He conveys the repulsive mixture of boredom, stupidity, filthiness, meanness, and chronic anxiety that is the prisoner's lot. The inmates are dysfunctional, the structure that houses them authoritarian. This book will scare you straight—or should. But within their cages, Dawkins's prisoners dream—of criminal schemes, drugs, women—and an American world outside the walls. Their avid fantasies burn with a furious light against the bleak institutional background, exploding with ingenuity, pathos, and rebellion. In many cases, these outsiders are, like Dawkins himself, artists."

—Atticus Lish, author of *Preparation for the Next Life*

"*The Graybar Hotel* is unlike any other short story collection I've ever read. Dawkins's cast of characters are forever longing for escape—escape from prison, escape from their past, escape from freedom, even. And when the escape is successful, when one reality is traded for another, Dawkins's characters find themselves lost, even pining for what they had in the first place. *The Graybar Hotel* is not a 'prison book.' It is a mirror, held up to our culture of incarceration. It is a testament, a testimony that the people inside prison are as much Americans, as much citizens as their guards, parole officers, and wardens, that there is no *outside*, that prisons are as much America as pubs, playgrounds, or parks. There is a current of electricity running through these stories, a shocking voltage of truth. What an authentic and rare book *The Graybar Hotel* is."

—Nickolas Butler, internationally bestselling author of *Shotgun Lovesongs*, *Beneath the Bonfire*, and *The Hearts of Men*

"The stories in *The Graybar Hotel* are astonishing, clever, and true. It's the best collection I've read in a long, long time."

—Roddy Doyle, author of *The Barrytown Trilogy* and the Booker Prize–winning *Paddy Clarke Ha Ha Ha*

THE GRAYBAR HOTEL

STORIES

CURTIS DAWKINS

SCRIBNER

New York London Toronto Sydney New Delhi

SCRIBNER
An Imprint of Simon & Schuster, Inc.
1230 Avenue of the Americas
New York, NY 10020

This book is a work of fiction. Any references to historical events, real people, or real places are used fictitiously. Other names, characters, places, and events are products of the author's imagination, and any resemblance to actual events or places or persons, living or dead, is entirely coincidental.

First Scribner trade paperback edition May 2018

Interior design by Kyle Kabel

Manufactured in the United States of America

1 3 5 7 9 10 8 6 4 2

Library of Congress Cataloging-in-Publication Data is available.

ISBN 978-1-5011-6229-9
ISBN 978-1-5011-6230-5 (pbk)
ISBN 978-1-5011-6231-2 (ebook)

To my people in Portland—
Kim, Henry, Elijah, and Lily Rose

CONTENTS

THE
GRAYBAR
HOTEL

Cold blood
flowing through the veins of
me and all my friends.
Still love
can be pumped out of our hearts.
This start might be the end.

—The Dears

COUNTY

Italian Tom was a saucier until a Cadillac doing sixty hit him and knocked the recipes out of his head. He had a faint line like an old smooth weld across the length of his forehead and the dark dots of suture scars. He wasn't five minutes in our cell before he knocked on the scar with his knuckles, making a dull metallic sound like he'd flicked an open can of soda with his finger. "Go ahead, try it," he said, taking a step closer.

"I heard it. I believe you," I said from my mat on the floor. Tom looked around our cell for another taker, but Domino and Ricky Brown were both sleeping.

Normally I'm not a very good conversationalist, but the past two months in jail had made clear to me I had nothing better to do. So if someone talked to me, I had resolved to take him up on it. At least until he got boring, or until the lies became too much, or until *The Price Is Right* came on. Since it was only 10:00 a.m. I said, "How long ago did it happen?"

"About fifteen years." Tom sat in quiet reflection on the

bench of our steel picnic table. "And the funny thing is, I was only visiting Cadillac for the day. My sister had begged me to come up there and meet her newest husband."

The television hadn't been turned on yet and Tom looked up through the bars to the cold, black screen we shared with the neighboring cell. I looked forward to seeing Bob Barker up there, and hearing Rod Roddy calling people to come on down. For an hour a day I could live in a world full of lights and color, noise and smiling women gracefully highlighting things with the near-touch of their hands. And hope. The hope for a good outcome kept me transfixed.

"Hold on," I said. "You were hit by a Cadillac *in* Cadillac?"

"Ain't that some shit?" Tom said. He turned away from the television and I could see his other scars then, some self-made, like the ones cut vertically through his eyebrows and the tiny notches in the rim of his right ear. "I was crossing the street to get a pint of gin and a pack of squares, then *bam!* Doing sixty in a twenty-five. Knocked me eighty feet and out of one of my sneakers."

"Now that's something I've never understood," I said. "I don't get how someone could be knocked out of their shoes. And your case is even more bizarre because you were only knocked out of one shoe."

"There were witnesses," Tom said. "That's how the cop figured out the speed the guy was going."

"What law of physics governs whether a person's shoe comes off?"

And what are the chances a person gets hit by a Cadillac in a town called Cadillac? I wondered. Did it mean that everything meant something? Even if that something is a lie? And who's in charge of the meaning? The liar? The lied to? And what the fuck could all of this possibly mean?

Ricky Brown woke up. He had been playing possum. Faking sleep becomes an art form in jail, especially when someone new comes in, and especially when he's asking you to knock on his skull.

"I'll tell you what it means," Ricky said from his bunk. He always had the uncanny ability to answer the questions that were floating around in my brain, as if we were both listening to the same party line but he had a better connection. "It means don't pay a lot of fucking money for tennis shoes. And it means life is a big, shiny machine made by General Motors, and it's a tale told by an idiot, signifying shit."

Ricky read a lot—Faulkner and Shakespeare mostly—so he thought he knew some things. He was a skinny, red-haired, old-school man with a tattoo of a court jester on his left arm and a green, faded wizard on his right. He had the giveaway constellation of a crack addict's scars on the insides of his wrists, the exact shape of a hot glass pipe hidden up inside his sleeves. Even without seeing his shins, I knew there would be scars there too, from the same pipe hidden in his socks.

"Yeah, yeah," Tom said. "Tale told by an idiot. Signifying shit. That's deep, man. I like that."

Kalamazoo is the Native American word for "boiling water." Rumor had it the county jail was built on an ancient hot spring filled in with loamy soil, and the whole building was slowly sinking as a result. After thirty-four years, the thought of Indian soil reclaiming the jail was nothing but a fairy tale, but that didn't stop anyone from talking about it after the television was turned off. The fantasy beat the reality. I would occasionally wake from dreams in which a ghostly chief, screaming in vengeance for his land, would split the building in half and we would all jump out and flee, racing on wild, galloping horses away from the jail as it was sucked down into the earth.

We were in A North wing, where the lights never went out. A North was suicide watch and though very few of us had actually tried to kill ourselves, we were all somehow a concern to the powers that be. I had never been to jail, and I was going to be locked up for a long time, so the county kept the high-watt rays of worried lights on me at all hours.

Along with the lights were the guards who walked past every seven minutes, like the steady sweep of a lighthouse beam. They would walk up to the bars, look in, and minus any scene of horror, they'd walk away without a word. Sometimes I'd ask about the weather, and sometimes they would answer, and it felt good to know that the outside was still there. But mostly the only way to get a guard's attention was to die, or press the panic button marked EMERGENCY ONLY in red, stenciled paint above the phone.

A North had eight cells—half held four inmates and the other half held six. But the jail was always overcrowded, so there was usually an extra man or two in each. I had been the fifth man in Cell 7, so I'd taken a mat on the floor in the dark corner by the door. Cellmates came and went, and I could have rightfully taken one of the bunks on the west wall, but as the methadone ran out I found comfort in the dimness of my corner. I lay there and sweat and shook, and tried not to think too much, and memorized the Twenty-third Psalm and recited it minute by minute, hour by hour.

I had Bob Barker every weekday morning, though. There were the games, the new cars, the spinning wheel, the showcases. Sometimes tears would fill my eyes when a lucky member of the audience would high-five their way through the crowd to stand on the contestant's row. They were so genuinely happy to be given a chance, and as they looked at Bob brightly lit onstage, it must have seemed like a better life was right there for the taking. Their hearts' desires were a possibility—and not in some distant future, but right then, or at least for the next hour. But Bob Barker and a screaming studio audience can only go so far as company, so by the time Italian Tom walked into A North 7, I guess I was ready.

Tom had moved on from talking about the hit-and-run to acting it out, standing up in the cell and moving in slow motion, like a marionette with joints held together by pins. He explained that, in fact, most of his bones and joints *were* metal, and he was only able to move freely after he'd been up and moving for a few hours, longer if the temperature was cold. "I'm still a little stiff," he said as he took off his shirt. It was January and only ten-thirty.

Tom's torso was half green with tattoos. After just a couple of months in jail, I'd learned to recognize tattoos inked in prison—they're green or gray and lack the sharp lines of a professional needle. Prison artists use whatever they have, usually a sharpened guitar string rigged to the motor of a cassette player. The ink is made of soot mixed with spit, sometimes urine, and the art, while brilliant and precise in concept, is dull and faded on the flesh. Tattooing in prison is like trying to sew fine stitches with a knitting needle. It's the essence of prison ingenuity—that so much can be done with so little.

Tom's chest looked like a page from an artist's sketch-pad—a couple old cars, a lion, Mickey Mouse, cell bars with tears spilling out, a green blob of something that may have been the Earth, or a ship, or a basketball, or the moon, and the full-body portrait of a woman Tom would later call Karen.

Karen was not a prison tattoo. She began over his heart and was clean and sharp with full, red lips. Her right eye closed in a wink, but the left iris was light green under long lashes. Her hair seemed blown by a wind up over Tom's left shoulder and neck, ending in wispy strands on his collarbone. She was nude, of course, with large breasts and wide hips straddling his sternum. Tom had a hairy Italian chest but had kept it shaved smooth and clean, everywhere except for Karen's pubic area, with its immaculately trimmed little triangle of hair.

The Price Is Right came and went but I could barely pay attention. I was watching the tattoo of Karen and wanting to touch her Italian olive skin. It felt awkward to stare at the chest of a man and fantasize about warmth and contact, but her light green eye and long, swirling hair seemed to speak to me, to have come down through the years since it was inked to grant me a moment's peace and connection to the human race.

The cell door opened and we were back up to six men. In walked a middle-aged, light-skinned black man with a misshapen afro and a patchy beard. Even in a fresh orange Kalamazoo County Jail jumpsuit he reeked of alcohol. "Ain't right. It ain't right," he said. "Mind my own business, cops come in and Taser my ass. That ain't right." He unbuttoned his jumpsuit halfway and rubbed at the two swollen marks from the Taser prongs, like a fresh snakebite. "And I'm hungry too, goddammit. That ain't right."

He was loud enough to wake Domino. The man paced the length of the cell, carrying on about the Taser sting until he saw Tom and his scar. "Damn, man!" he said. "What happened to you? You get shot or something?"

"I got hit by a Caddy doing sixty."

"You look like Frankenstein, man. You should be dead."

"I did die—twice," said Tom, "but they shocked me

back to life." He knocked again on the metal plates in his forehead. "This is all steel."

"Then you *is* Frankenstein!" the man said, and went back to pacing and complaining about his hunger and police brutality.

Tom's face and shoulders sank, like whoever had been pulling his strings had just dropped them. He looked at the drunk for a second, then looked down, and it was amazing to see a man so big hurt by something so small. But in here you can't just shoot down a man and his story, lie or not. What's more, he'd called Tom a monster, and even Frankenstein has feelings.

"You know," Tom said, "if you're hungry you can get something to eat."

"Yeah, how?"

"Go push that button up there on the wall and order a pizza."

The man walked over to the corner of the cell. "It says 'Emergency Only.'"

"If hunger's not an emergency, man, I don't know what is."

"Yeah, okay!" said the drunk. "What you guys want on it? I'll share." He put his finger on the button. "Man, they don't do shit like this in the Kent County."

A woman's voice came over the intercom: "What's the problem?"

"I'm hungry," the drunk said. "I want to order a pizza."

"Hold on," she said.

He looked back at us, giddy, like a would-be big

shot handing out money not his own. "So you guys like pepperoni?"

All of us nodded in our own slight ways. Then the lock of the heavy steel door slid open and five guards stepped straight for him.

"Okay, smart-ass, we'll get you your pizza," said a bald guard with a mustache. The drunk was handcuffed and dragged out of the cell before he even had time to grasp what was happening. He looked puzzled as he left, as if he was still expecting them to ask what toppings he wanted.

Afternoons, during soap operas, we would mute the TV and read, write letters, do whatever it took to pass the four hours until dinner.

Tom made his bed, then sat at the picnic table to draw. I lay on my mat in the corner and watched the silent soap opera figures on the television screen. There was a ransom plot going on that week—a gorgeous blonde tied to a chair in a storage facility. Without ever hearing the words the characters spoke, I'd noticed a dark trend toward kidnapping that month on daytime drama.

At the table, Tom hummed, tapped his pen, and drew. I got up and sat across from him. The edges of the page he worked on were adorned with roses, thorny stems, and leaves, and the middle looked to have a poem or song printed on it.

"Thought I'd see what you were working on," I said.

"It's my hustle back in the joint." His was a common

one for artistic types who get locked up—selling drawings and poems for others to send home.

"But here's the deal, right?" said Tom. "Here's my new angle—gay, erotic rap songs. Don't get me wrong, I ain't gay or nothing, but I can't wait to get back to prison. I'm gonna clean up. It's an untapped market."

"So who's the lady?" I asked, nodding to the tattoo on his chest.

"Karen," he said. "Karen Sharon. She was my girl a long time ago, back before Cadillac. I used to have a lot of girls before that shit."

Tom looked down at his page and nodded his head to the beat of his tapping pen. He continued drawing and I stared at the little details that made up Karen Sharon: her red lips, the long, clean neck, the slight rib lines below her breasts, then the wide, soft hips. There was that small patch of pubic hair, her knees, calves, and finally her thin ankles and dainty feet. The long hair that wrapped around Tom's neck seemed curlier up close, less like a flowing river. Again, I felt the urge to reach across the table and touch her. She seemed so alive, like if I jabbed my finger at her open eye, she might reflexively close it.

She must have been a shallow woman to leave him after the accident. Then again, he probably wasn't a model boyfriend either. I could have been projecting, though. Like all of us who'd wasted our time out there, he'd no doubt taken his life and relationships for granted. Now he was a man who couldn't wait to get back to prison and make a killing in the gay rap market.

The soap opera—I think it was the one with the big hourglass—was ending. The kidnapped lady in the storage facility was about to die from a fire deliberately set by some contraption involving gasoline, dirty rags, and an alarm clock. The scene faded from a close-up of the ticking clock to a handsome couple toasting each other with champagne in a hotel bar. Then the credits rolled, and the sand slid through the hourglass again.

The next day I woke to Tom tapping his pen in some rhythm, occasionally looking up at the TV as if searching for rhymes for his gay rap. Volunteers from a nearby church brought by the squeaky book cart. Ricky picked an ancient-looking paperback and began reading it on his bunk. Domino woke up for a minute only to try to call someone on the phone.

I spent the morning waiting for the soap opera to come back on. And of course, the kidnapped lady left for certain death did not die. I knew she wouldn't, so few of them ever do. It was the means of her escape I was waiting for. And at the last minute, she cut away the ropes with the prongs of her wedding ring, then ran out of the storage facility just seconds before the place was engulfed in flame. The beautiful couple in the hotel bar was arrested; the victim led the cops right to them and she smiled as they were cuffed. Through it all, she had only a dark smudge of soot on her cheek.

On the whole, it was a good day on TV. Earlier, a

blue-haired old lady won thirty grand playing Plinko on *The Price Is Right*, then went on to win both showcases. At four o'clock, *Oprah* came on. Domino slept, but Tom, Ricky, and I watched Tracey Gold, former television star, recount her harrowing drunk-driving accident and arrest. "I didn't even know I was drunk," she said.

"Me neither," said Ricky. "Let me out."

In a later segment Oprah showed her audience that the one glass of wine they might have while playing cards at a friend's house was actually equivalent to three shots of whiskey—because the glass of wine was filled to the top. "So watch out," Oprah warned.

"Shit," said Ricky. "Drunk-ass Tracey Gold damn near kills her kids in that wreck, and all I did was smoke a rock. I should be on *Oprah,* not in fucking jail."

"Ain't that some shit?" Tom said. We all nodded in agreement. It *was* some shit all right, though I'm sure we all had different ideas about what exactly that shit was.

The food in jail was usually good, and that night we enjoyed the best Kalamazoo County had to offer: chunks of dark-meat turkey stir-fried with vegetables in a soy sauce gravy. I watched Tom stir the tip of his spoon in the sauce, like he was mixing oil paint for a portrait. First he sniffed it, then he dabbed some on his tongue. "This cook really knows what she's doing," Tom said. "Just enough garlic and allspice."

I wondered how Tom knew that the cook was a woman, and as always, Ricky came on cue. "How do you know a lady made it?"

"Come on," Tom said. "Because it's softer, warmer. It's obvious. You taste things like that when you slow it down a little."

"The fuck you mean slow it down?"

"I mean really taste it," Tom said. "Close your eyes if you have to. Nobody tastes anything anymore. They just shovel, shovel, shovel. But man, food is just like wine—hold it in your mouth and concentrate, you can seriously taste the terroir of the ingredients."

"Terr-what?" I asked.

"The taste of the land where the ingredients were grown."

Ricky took a bite and smiled. "I taste something, all right. It tastes like a field and hay."

"Yeah," I said. "And a barn."

"I think you guys are really getting it," said Tom.

"And cows," Ricky said. "At least what comes out of cows—very definitely some bullshit."

Tom smiled. "Seriously, though. Maybe you can't, but I can taste all those things. I can taste the earth that grew it, and I can taste the prayers of the lady who made it for us."

The idea that someone might be praying for us shut us up and we ate. I tried to taste the softness Tom talked about, and prayers inside our sauce. Domino ate his quickly so he could go back to sleep.

The guard took our trays and I guess Tom figured he had a good seven minutes to get it done. He took the top linen sheet off his bunk and began twisting it into a rope. "Well, fellas," he said, "I'm checking out of the K'zoo motel. I've had enough of this county shit—a man needs a coffee and cigarette after a meal like that. So after that guard walks past again, I'm going to sling this sheet up and get myself back to the joint. Once I'm up there, just hit the panic button."

Tom sat shirtless on the picnic table bench and looped the end of the sheet onto itself. Karen Sharon moved and swayed as he worked; she seemed to gyrate with every pulse of his muscles as he tied the noose. Tom threw the sheet on his bunk. I felt nerves tingle in my hands and feet.

"If you on parole, you're going back in a month anyway," said Ricky. "You ain't got to pull this fool shit over a cigarette."

Tom either didn't hear him or pretended not to hear. He glanced toward the bars and listened for the guard's footsteps. I told myself the whole fake suicide would be just that and nothing more—it would go smoothly, and in just a few minutes, Tom would be gone and our cell would be peaceful again.

The guard stepped past and barely glanced inside. Tom picked up the sheet from his bunk. "Nice knowing you guys," he said. He stood on the edge of the bench and tied the free end of his sheet around one of the long, horizontal slats of steel. He climbed up to the third steel slat, put the noose around his neck, and held on with a hand behind his back. With the lights behind him, all his green tattoos became dark, muddied blotches, and even Karen Sharon looked instantly older. I could see her as she was, after years of alcohol abuse and living with her shallow soul.

"Okay," Tom said. "Hit it."

Ricky and I didn't move. Domino sat up and looked. The heels of Tom's jail-issued flip-flops were wedged between the bars. Tom tightened the noose, then looked at each of us and let go with the hand behind his back. The top half of his body inched away from the bars, the brunt of his weight still held by his heels. The noose tightened, and his face turned red.

"Come on, you motherfuckers, hit the button."

One foot at a time, Tom kicked the flip-flops off. They each landed on the floor with a slap. He stepped off the flat steel that was holding his weight and began to die. The muscles in his chest convulsed and Karen began to dance again—ugly and desperate—an aging stripper, a whore. Tom's struggling seemed to reveal her true self, shedding layers of beauty and falseness. I didn't look away, though; I still wanted to touch her. I didn't care what she was as long as she would touch me back. And she would, I knew—I saw it in her eyes, in the split second when her closed eye opened, then shut again in a wink meant only for me.

I got off the bench, put my arms around Tom's legs, and lifted him with my shoulder.

"Don't touch me, don't touch me," he gasped.

Ricky walked over and hit the panic button.

"What's the problem?" the woman's voice asked.

"Some fool's trying to hang hisself."

Italian Tom pissed his orange pants and the warmth covered my shoulder. In a matter of seconds, the door slammed open and several guards entered. A female guard climbed the bars and cut the sheet with industrial scissors. Tom and I fell to the floor and the breath left my chest as my head struck the metal edge of the picnic table, then the concrete floor. She cut the noose from around his neck, and I heard his gasp for breath and could feel it as if it were my own. I could feel his sad life on top of me and it was suffocating.

The guards worked to stabilize Tom's neck as I lay there feeling the cold floor growing warmer with the wetness flowing from my head. I felt myself softening, sinking into the hot springs beneath Kalamazoo.

I tried to sit up but the female officer put her hand gently on my forehead to keep me down. She kneeled in front of me, close enough that I could smell her herbal shampoo. I looked at her name tag, "Lillie." I wanted to ask if that was her first or last name. I wanted to ask her: Do you like to watch snow come down late at night? When did your parents divorce? What's your favorite movie? Do you cry when you don't get mail for a long time? Would you want to be president? Are you happy? Do you hate the news? Does the sight of a jet slicing through the cold, thin air break your heart?

But I couldn't speak. I was afraid that if I spoke, she'd take her hands from my body. So I lay there and looked at Lillie as the water began to boil and the horses started to run.

A HUMAN NUMBER

The first person I talked to was Kitty-Kat. Kitty-Kat didn't sound like a Kitty-Kat though, he sounded old and gruff, as if he'd drunk whiskey like water for fifty years. I wrote his number near the dozens of others on the wall next to the phone, but when I woke from a nap the walls were covered with a fresh layer of paint, a pale green over the original orange—like an old bruise or gangrenous flesh.

After Kitty-Kat it was a week before I could get anyone else. I started writing down the numbers in the phone book, on a big ad in the yellow pages for Ritter's Family Photos. There was no family in the ad, just a house in a valley and a windmill on a hill and a sheep grazing in the front pasture. I wrote the numbers in the open sky above the windmill.

Who is this?

Hey, it's me, I say. You're supposed to record your name, so when the person picks up, the generic computer operator asks if you will accept a call from so-and-so from jail. Mine says, Hey, it's me. Just something I came up with. Not many people know someone with my name, but everyone knows a me.

Heyitsme could be anyone. Some long-missing son, a forgotten uncle, your addict cousin written off as hopeless.

Who is this?

Who is this?

They have to press 1 to accept the charges, spending $2.40 for the first minute, and $0.27 every minute after that, up to fifteen minutes total. Six eighteen is just enough money that during a dead stretch, I worry that no one might answer again.

She read for a long time from Revelation, an old lady with a soft, slow voice: *Then I looked, and behold, a Lamb . . . And I heard a voice from heaven . . . These are the ones who were not defiled with women . . . And I saw another angel flying in the midst of heaven . . . And the smoke of their torment ascends forever and ever . . . Whoever receives the mark of his name . . . and behold, a white cloud . . . And something like a sea of glass mingled with fire . . . Let him who hath understanding reckon the number of the beast, for it is a human number . . . I stood on the sand of the sea and saw a beast rising up out of the sea, having seven heads and ten horns . . . The beast I saw was . . .*

I could barely hear her over the two men at our stainless-steel table talking about the inventions that would make them rich when they got out:

1. A desire-transfusion machine that trades an imminent suicide's wish to die with a terminally ill person's desire to live. They believed it might be as easy as switching the two people's blood.
2. Home simple-surgery kits.
3. Anti-tornado bombs.

Little D said from the shower, Thems the dumbest ideas I ever heard.

But I don't know.

Who is this?

Hey, it's me.

I don't know nobody in prison.

I'm not in prison yet. I'm in jail. The two are very different, but people think they're the same.

Why'd you call?

I'm bored.

So am I. I don't know what to do with myself since I retired.

What did you retire from?

Had my own auto body shop. Insurance work. Paint and detailing. Or I'd buy totaled cars real cheap and then go and straighten the frame, rebuild it from scratch, basically—pretty good money in that, taking them to the auction. But I had a heart attack and a bypass, so I sold it. Now my wife and me breed these fancy chickens that lay blue eggs.

That sounds nice.

I guess. We're starting to hate each other. My wife and me. About as much as I hate those friggin' chickens. I told her, if I can't work no more then she's gonna have to get a job, get out of the house during the day. Or I might end up right there with you.

He went on like that for the length of the call, as if we were old friends and he was catching me up on the things I'd missed. He confided that he was thinking about taking up smoking again, despite, or because of, his heart. Either that, or grow roses. Before the line disconnected, I heard his wife enter the room.

Who you talking to? she said.

I have no idear, he said. You want to talk to him? Tell him about your goddamn designer chickens?

I heard the phone move away from his mouth and the silence as he held it out to his wife, just before our time was up and the line clicked dead.

People love to talk—that's why they answer. I try to listen past their voice and into their home, to the world around them. What TV show is playing? What pets are running around? I once heard a parakeet squawking, "He's buried in the sandbox." I listen for the traffic outside, a neighbor playing piano. Once, in a senior assisted-living building, I heard a xylophone being hammered in expert scales. Countless layers of sound make up the world, and I hear it all: voices; vacuuming; traffic through an open window; the hum of washers, dryers, refrigerators, all so slight the sound is barely perceptible.

Kitty-Kat had a busted knee. He said he answered my call because he'd once spent a weekend right where I was—he was drunk and took a swing at his brother-in-law, missed him and coldcocked his sister. What was I there for? he wondered, but never asked me outright. Mostly, he just went on about the right way to roof a house since energy costs were skyrocketing.

He was on Vicodin for the knee, which he hadn't busted on a roofing job like everyone assumed, but getting out of his Dodge Ram outside his house. He just stepped off the curb and twisted his ankle, which ended up internally screwing up that shit knee. He kept calling it that—that shit knee, like a foreign word he'd learned at war.

He didn't know the name of the surgery he'd had on that shit knee, but it was done with wires thinner than human hair. And under the local anesthetic he could hear the lasers hum and watch them flicker red, like police strobes glinting off the polished silver of the surgical light. He wondered if he should have been wearing some sort of welder's goggles, or at least sunglasses or something, you know, for eye protection. Well guess what, he said, he was going to keep an eye out (ha ha) for any future problems with his sight, and then sue those big-shot bastards into the Stone Age.

Had I ever seen *The Six Million Dollar Man*? You know, with Lee Majors? He'd told people that with all the lasers and the tiny titanium additions, and the round of cortico-what-have-you-steroids, he was part bionic. Not six million dollars bionic, but about ten grand bionic.

He'd said to call back anytime. But his number was gone under that sickly green. This was before I got my pen, a jail-approved ballpoint given to us by the Gideons. The pen was a slender, ink-filled insert wrapped in a thin tube, flexible, so you couldn't stab anyone with it. We called them "broke dicks."

I've always felt guilty for not calling Kitty-Kat again, like I've hurt his feelings. I try it every day, 349-something.

349-1234: The person at the number you dialed did not accept, or the call was received by an automated answering device.

349-1235: The person at the number you dialed did not . . .

349-1236: The number you dialed is a nonworking number.

I don't have certain numbers to call, you see. I have every number.

349-1238: The number you dialed is a nonworking number.

349-1239: The number you dialed is a nonworking number.

Tomorrow I'll start with 1240.

Oh, I'm so glad you called. I was just thinking of you. Now where were we— After these things I looked, and behold the temple of the tabernacle of the testimony was opened in heaven . . . and she did not repent . . . I will kill her children with death . . . I will give to each one of you according to your works— Oh, wait just a minute, son, my pie is done.

She put the phone down, I imagined, on the kitchen table, and I heard the oven door open and heard her praising the pie's flakiness and aroma, the simple perfection of it. And through the phone I could smell the hot, sticky blackberries and the golden crust. I heard the song of a grandfather clock and a semi rumbling past. I closed my eyes and sat at the table in the kitchen of this old lady who loved to tell me about the end of the world in her sweet old-lady voice.

I think she forgot about me, which was perfect. I listened to her hum some tunes I didn't recognize, and she talked to her blackberry pie as if it was a small child or a puppy: "Oh, you are a nice little yummy thing, aren't you. You are just perfect . . ."

The computer-voiced operator cut in—you have one minute remaining. Sometimes that minute seems long and drawn-out, and sometimes it is over much too quickly. "You are a little golden circle of sunshine, aren't you—" and the connection ended.

I hung up just as a skinny, black, effeminate man called Peanut came into the cell, looked around, then fell to the floor and had a seizure. The deputies rolled him in a wheelchair down to the nurse. He returned about an hour later and we were all nervous, thinking every noise was Peanut falling to the floor again. Little D said we were all seizure-shy, like a nervous dog forever jumping at loud noises. I took my seat at the phone.

This call is from Heyitsme at the Kalamazoo County Jail. It is subject to monitoring and recording. Thank you for using Global Tel Link.

Who is this? Fuck it—never mind. *Lone Ranger*'s on. You ever watch this shit? This geezer channel shows 'em every goddamn afternoon. The original one. The black-and-white one, not the later bullshit ones. You know those ones where he wasn't allowed to wear his goddamned mask? He had to wear sunglasses because the mask is trademarked or some shit. You believe that fucking political correctness nowadays? Everybody's feelings—turning us into a nation of pussies.

It's probably a legal issue, I said. Trademarks and stuff.

No, it's all bullshit, man. We're a nation of pussies, mired in bullshit.

A lot of people here watch that station, if that tells you anything.

Who does? The police or the jailbirds? Fuck that anyway. Listen—I'm going to my niece's first communion at Saint Jude's this weekend, even though they didn't invite me. Bunch of bastards. Body of Christ. That priest has always had it out for me. She's in the second grade, my niece.

What's your phone number there?

Why? You're the one who called me.

I know, but I keep forgetting to write down the numbers. Most of these numbers don't work, and when they do work I get wrapped up in talking, then forget.

Fine. 349-1302. Did you write it down? Just don't call me all the time, dude. But call sometimes. Next time I'll tell you how I knew Lance Armstrong was doping because he had cancer in his balls. Just common sense, man.

I will.

Now listen—I've been waiting to tell this to someone and you called right on time. I'm at the mall, right? I'm at the bus stop outside Ruby Tuesday's at Crossroads mall and this fat, old, bearded guy sits next to me, making small talk about what brought me to the mall, the gorgeous weather, the Tigers' prospects, and the high cost of gas and whatever. So, what do you do for fun? he says.

And I tell him, I like to hunt.

Oh, wonderful, he says. What do you hunt—dove, rabbit, deer?

And I look right at him and say: Fat, white, bearded bastards.

Peanut walked around our cell in a sort of daze that one of the deputies said was malingering with the intent of getting sent to the hospital. He would Malinger With Intent around our four-man cell saying what people say when they answer a call from the county jail. Who is this? he would say. Who is this?

I was jealous that Peanut was said to be Malingering With Intent. It really sounded like something to be.

For the time is at hand! He who is unjust, let him be unjust still; he who is filthy, let him be filthy still; he who is righteous, let him be righteous still; he who is holy . . . I am the Alpha and the Omega, the Beginning and the End, the First and the Last . . . The grace of our Lord Jesus Christ be with you all. Amen. And that, my friend, is the end of the Bible. It's like the whole thing is a very long prayer, how it ends with Amen. You get that?

I did. But how does it begin?

It's a fucking assault on the Second Amendment, is what it is. If they can take away the Lone Ranger's mask, they can, and will, take our guns. That doesn't mean shit to you, but you might want to know what's going on out here. I know a couple of militia types, and they are crazy. But Timothy McVeigh, he was framed, you know. A patsy.

There was silence between us for a minute. I could hear a television commercial in the background: *Drive a Ferrari like the rich and famous . . .*

And then he changed, like a station on TV.

I'm going to come and get you, kid. I fucking swear to God. You're in there thinking, How's he going to do that? He don't know where I lock, he don't know my name. But I got ways. It's easier than hell to get in there—you know that already. It's getting out that's hard.

Here's what I'll do: at my niece's fancy fucking communion, I'm going to punch the priest and get put in a cell with you, and then I'm going to eat you up like a greasy soup. And while I'm gobbling you up, I'll tell you how I found you, Mr. Heyitsme. Just kidding, I won't tell you shit. But I'll be there next week. Or tomorrow. Body of Christ and all that. Body of you. Amen.

Who is this?

Who is this?

They took Peanut to the nurse again. When he came back there was a cotton ball taped into the crook of his left arm. The next morning the cotton ball lay on the floor, a drop of blackened blood staring up like a pupil in a big white eye. No one picked it up—we didn't want to catch what he had, whatever it was.

Peanut started gagging and gurgling in between his whispering. Who is this? Who is this? And I figured out he probably wasn't saying Who is this, but something like Do his bit, or Knew this shit, or, You missed it. After a while it started to infect my head, and to combat Peanut's refrain, I would say to myself: malingering with intent, malingering with intent, malingering with intent.

Peanut walked two or three circles around the table,

then flopped to the floor and someone hit the panic button above the wall-mounted phone. The nurses came in blue scrubs and carried equipment in tackle boxes, looking as if they were on their way to a costume party at a fishing pond. Peanut held his stomach and lurched into and out of a fetal position. He stared vacantly at the wall while the nurses took his blood pressure, pulse rate, et cetera.

I sat at the table watching. You never know when you might need malingering skills, and if Peanut *was* only malingering, he was really good at it. I was an understudy apprenticed to a master. They wheeled him away, leaving a quarter-size puddle of shiny drool on the floor, which I swept away with a swipe of my flip-flop. Before the streak was completely dry, Peanut walked in again.

I was on the phone trying to find Kitty-Kat when I heard the commercial on TV: *Avoid disappointment and future regret—call today.* I listened to the info, hung up, and dialed the toll-free number. It was some sort of gold commemorative buffalo coin.

It rang twice, then stopped. American Majesty Keepsakes, she said, How can I help you?

I'm in jail, I said.

Yeah, I heard the machine. My brother's in jail. I get this call pretty often, though not at work.

I would like to see about getting the coin that prevents disappointment and future regret.

It's $19.95, payable by credit card or electronic check. Sorry, no CODs.

That's a pretty good deal for all it promises.

The $19.95 includes shipping and handling. You can get a free one—actually, I'll be honest, you *have* to get the free one—for extra shipping and handling. It ends up coming to about forty dollars.

Forty? I can't really afford that.

Well, you can't really order anything from jail, anyway. You might as well be on the moon.

For a few days, Peanut moaned and held his stomach. He told the deputy he was pregnant. The deputy walked away, talking on her noisy walkie-talkie, which squeaked and chirped at all hours like a caged monkey. Peanut sat at the table and rocked back and forth. He said he was having a miscarriage or something.

Probably gas, Little D said, hopefully, as if by diagnosing the problem Peanut's troubles would end and he would shut up and we could all quit wondering what sort of malingering nonsense we were going to have to listen to next.

But in the corner of the cell, Little D confided quietly to me: He might really have something. Like rabies, or AIDS, or syphilis. You better think fast if he tries to bite you.

I gave him a look of disbelief.

I'm just saying, he said. Just kick at him—psychos don't like to be kicked.

I hit a cold streak on the phone. Several days without a connection. I'd been desperate before and called lawyers—not lawyers exactly, but the receptionists—all of them cynically polite at first, until they determine whether or not you are going to make the firm any money. Usually I hear typing and voices in the background, the busy sounds of a bustling office. Once I said I was the victim of a drug company's negligence, in jail because corporate goons had framed me.

What medication were you on?

Viagra, I said, which got me fast-tracked to a phone interview with an attorney.

So, what happened with the Viagra? a male voice said.

I got an erection, I said.

That's what's supposed to happen.

I hesitated a moment, and heard him sigh before hanging up.

The bail bondsmen you can actually talk to. Or their secretaries if they have one. But more often than not bondsmen are depressing, one-man operations. They'll listen awhile because technically I could be bailed out, if I had collateral or someone to put collateral up. Or maybe they listen because bail bondspeople are low down on the justice system totem pole, one step above security guards. They never aspired to get accused criminals out on bail. Life didn't work out somehow, and the failure translates to a willingness to listen a few minutes, even chat a little. They'll ask where you're locked, how long you've been there, how it's going. They pretend to care long after it's obvious there's no money to be had in you.

Who is this?

Retired men are the most likely to answer, followed by elderly widows. Followed by former inmates, then their family members.

Do I know you? they sometimes ask. I know you, don't I?

I tell them, It depends on what you mean by *know.*

A voice came over the intercom—not unlike the generic, computer-voiced, Global Tel Link operator: I had a visitor. Who? I said. Marvin Newhouse, she said.

I didn't know any Marvin, but I was thinking maybe Kitty-Kat found me, or the guy crashing his niece's first communion. I buttoned up my orange jumpsuit. I combed my hair. Peanut was on the toilet, moaning. Little D said he was pooping out his baby. I left the cell and followed the deputy to the visitation room, six partitioned windows with phones where you stand to talk.

It's a long, narrow room that's always hot from the previous inmates' body heat, and it smells like a rotting garden hose. I stood at the far window and cleaned the black phone receiver with the front of my jumpsuit. The visitors filed in: middle-aged women with breasts bulging from their button-up shirts like dough rising; a man with a Bible; two younger ladies with the same rising loaves, this time over the sides of their jeans.

Marvin, whoever he was, never showed. I stood there in my own chest-high cubicle with the phone up to my ear wondering who was supposed to be standing in front of me. Whoever it was, at that moment, was walking across the parking lot to their car, putting the key in the ignition, driving away with one last look, like the place was a national monument.

I listened to the mingled hum of the voices on my side of the room and studied my partial reflection in the smudged glass. I could see cloudy outlines of hands and lips, all getting smaller in size farther down the window. I was looking at myself, of course, a transparent portrait brushstroked in greasy smears, but I imagined my friend, Kitty-Kat.

I laughed a good laugh, glad to see him. His knee was doing a lot better, he said, but now he thought he might be addicted to Vicodin.

I laughed again, then apologized, because addiction's nothing to laugh at. I told him about the madman who was going to crash his niece's communion, how I had been watching the local news expecting to hear about some dustup at a Catholic church.

I laughed it off, but Kitty-Kat grew worried. He said he would talk to a deputy, an old high school buddy of his, and maybe get some extra protection for me. I was a worthwhile person, he said. I wasn't damaged, or diminished or anything just for the mistakes I'd made, and seemed to keep making. What would happen is this: in certain people, failure could turn into an asset. Failure could make you a better person. It could turn into success.

We stared in silence a moment through the bullet-proof glass. I brought up a new subject to wipe away the silence: Peanut, and his constant antics, about him on the toilet getting rid of his baby. I talked about the inventions those guys at the table had come up with. He said I would really have some stories to tell some-day, and all I needed was a stable home and steady job like roofing to really flourish. I felt like he was going to ask me to come and live with him when I got out, help him around the house while his knee healed. But the deputy came in and said time was up, we had to head back. I laughed one last time before following the others out of the hot, narrow room, adding my echoes to the millions already there—thicker and thicker with each new gangrened layer.

On my way back, I had a number in my mind. I could see it as clearly as if it had appeared in the smudged window, written in dull, oily numerals, as if Kitty-Kat had said it out loud, and I repeated it over and over, making sure not to forget it before I could write it down.

I got that broke dick pen and wrote down the num-ber on my mattress, in a little space on the end that my sheet didn't cover. 349-1568. I mumbled it to myself even afterward, hoping I would never forget it again.

Little D said, You gonna start with that psycho shit now that he's gone?

What?

You notice anything different?

I looked around the cell.

Peanut's gone, I said. What happened?

I told you he had something, didn't I?

It hadn't been rabies, or anything like that. Peanut really had been pregnant. She was a woman impersonating a man. She was wanted, as a woman, for a long list of nationwide financial crimes involving an Internet charity kidney transplant scam. The nurse told Little D that the pregnancy was probably an echo-something, something where the egg gets caught in the Philippine tube.

Can you fucking believe that? said Little D.

I bet those deputies feel like idiots.

They're used to it by now.

It was all too much. Too much at once, I thought. I had to tell someone. I picked up the receiver and put it to my ear, still warm from the visiting room. Press 0 for a collect call, the operator said. I pressed 0, then the number I had visualized. I waited.

I was going to tell him about Marvin Newhouse, how I knew it was him. I would tell him about Peanut, and I'd tell him that this time I had saved the number on the end of my mattress, and tomorrow when I called, he wouldn't ask Who is it? He'd say, Hey, I know you.

I know you, he'll say, and we'll talk about Vicodin and roofing. We'll talk about shit knees and madmen, first communions and the end of the world. I have a lot to say. But first he has to answer.

Answer, I whispered into the phone. Answer.

SUNSHINE

George had come back from the visiting room where his girlfriend, Sunshine, just told him she had cancer. He couldn't touch her or hold her, of course, through the phone, through the glass. He said he almost tried to smash through the thick, shatterproof pane, but he figured he'd be tackled long before he ever got to comfort her. He looked around at us with the anger still in his eyes, as if expecting praise for his restraint from trying something that would have been impossible to begin with.

Just down the hall was a cell of suicidal women who wrote dirty notes on little bars of soap, then slid them down to our cell, like illicit Olympic curlers. No matter the gender, all the suicide cases were lumped in this one small section of the jail. We never laid eyes on the women, only heard them and read their notes. The men in general population probably would have loved to be so close to women, but it was frustrating and meaningless, and I would've traded them ten times over for a better TV to replace ours, which was slowly dying up on the wall. Half the time there was only a black screen and the voices inside, or an occasional haunting thump from the speaker.

No one died on the suicide watch wing when I was there. A man did commit suicide over in the jail, but he wasn't on A North, he was in segregation. My wife came to visit on the same day jail officials gave his personal belongings to his grieving sister in the waiting room. My wife didn't go into detail about it; she was shaken and I didn't press. But in my mind I've played that scene over and over again. I imagine a sibling, someone I love and grew up with, who goes to jail—which is bad enough—but then the personal demons set in and I never see them alive again. I clutch a paper bag of their things that doesn't seem to weigh enough.

On A North, no one died. None of us, at least. But George's girlfriend had cancer and we all felt horrible about it. When you're separated from the people you know and love, every emotion is multiplied. Your mind becomes a very clear prism, into which every feeling enters, then becomes seven or eight different shades. We were all responsible for being there, of course—none of us were innocent. But that only makes you feel worse when you're the one in jail.

We were sad about Sunshine, and we were worried about George, who was a surly kid who would fight anyone at the drop of a hat. Finding out about the cancer didn't help his already touchy mood. I had been making chess pieces from wet toilet paper, and was just about finished with the bishops, which strongly resembled the pawns. George sat on his bunk and said, Her hair was falling out. And then he started to cry. I mean he really cried. Sobbing.

How long has she had cancer? one of us asked.

She just—sob—found out—sob—today.

And of course, being the resident know-it-all, I explained to George that something was strange about Sunshine's cancer story. No one's hair falls out the same day they're diagnosed with cancer.

That's the chemo, I said. And if they just found it, she couldn't have started chemo yet.

George always had a problem with violence—it was the first thing he said when he became the fifth man in our cell. He said his father used to set up fights between him and his drinking buddies' kids. They would place bets, like the kids were roosters or dogs. I expected to be punched after I'd basically called Sunshine a liar. But I wasn't punched. I just kept adding my wet wads of toilet paper to build up the bishops.

George stopped sobbing. He lay back on his bunk and listened to the black TV as if he could see what was happening there.

I always assumed it was Sunshine who was the liar—that she'd been diagnosed months earlier but had to work up the nerve to tell him face-to-face. But years after I was on A North with George, it occurred to me that it was probably him who had made the whole story up. For sympathy, or something like it.

He lay there watching the black screen and seemed to really enjoy the soap opera that was going on. It was like a radio play, or eavesdropping, as if the action were taking place just on the other side of our cinder-block wall. There was a hostage situation—some nut with a Southern accent demanding a couple million in ransom. We could hear that the hostage was a regular character, so we knew no permanent damage would be done. She might think she was going to die, but there was no way she would. In fact, the situation might do the spoiled twerp some good. It might deepen her shallow soul. Then there was a loud thump from the speaker and a wisp of smoke rose from the back of the TV. And that was it. The television died a slightly smoky death.

We never learned how the hostage situation turned out, if it affected the soap opera's character or not. I imagine it gave her nightmares, as proximity to death is wont to do, and like me she wakes up in a paper bag, waiting on someone to pick them up.

DAYTIME DRAMA

Arthur wore a cape in the county jail. He fashioned it from the dark gray wool blanket given to each inmate, and the knot from the tied corners rested on his Adam's apple. November was a cold one in the jail and the cape kept him warm, plus the dark, brooding superhero effect was not lost on Arthur. He looked at himself in the dull, scratched metal mirror above the stainless-steel toilet, flashed a toothless grin, then turned around with a swoop and sat at the steel picnic table bolted to the floor of our cell.

The other three men slept. The television on the wall was dark, silent, and dusty. There was a thick, dingy window to the left of the TV, and the first rays of the day cut a shaft of light through the cell, lighting the corner.

He wanted to do some push-ups. He could feel one of the guys watching him, so it was a show of primal strength that, despite some extra pounds, he was much stronger than the average man. Not in the middle of the room, though—too obvious that he was putting on a show. In the space between the bench seat and the wall instead. It was a tight fit, but he would make it work. He closed his eyes and thought a moment. He thought of the strength running through his blood, his veins, rushing through his chest and arms. He wondered why they took his fucking false teeth. Fucking fuckers. That was good. Rage was good. Watch this.

"What are you doing?"

"Praying."

"Looks like you were trying to do a push-up."

"Nope." Arthur glanced up. Don't stare, though, not at first. But what in the hell was that flicker? Like he's got a candle in his mouth. No white guy could pull it off; it's the dark skin that makes it pop, like stars in the night.

Arthur stood. "Can I see your teeth?" He also really liked the young man's hair, neatly braided and laid in rows with the ends in short rubber-banded ponytails.

"You want my teeth? You gone give me the eggs off your breakfast tray?"

"Deal," Arthur said, and went over to the young man. The other two men slept soundly. The teeth were crystal clear and the young man clicked them together several times, creating a sound like a wooden cane tapped against the floor. The front two teeth were inlaid with gold, initials CJ.

"Can I try 'em out?"

"Where's your grill?"

"They took them."

"Why?"

"I don't know. They're just plain white, though. I didn't even know you could get teeth like that. How much did they cost you?"

"Two," the young man said.

"Two hundred?" It was the wrong answer, Arthur knew. He felt very white.

"Two thousand," the young man said, and suddenly Arthur was back in Manhattan again. There was a narrow brick building on Orchard Street in Chinatown that manufactured Chinese sausage. Ten-foot strands of red, raw meat twisted into links every six inches hung in the window. Even in the cell Arthur could smell the gin they used. Around noon the laborers lined the counter, picking thick noodles from chicken broth with chopsticks. On the street he could hear the Jews five doors down, talking to passersby, asking them to come into their store and try on a shirt.

Two thousand sausage links hung in the window. Had to be. But the lady came out and said, "You go now." And he did, because he didn't have to count them anymore—he knew. And when the Jewish man with psoriasis on his forehead grabbed his elbow and said, "Come in," Arthur did. The man measured the width of Arthur's shoulders and slipped on a dark gray knee-length coat handmade in Italy. The sleeves were too long, but could be tailored, the man said. Still, in the mirror Arthur saw a young man—a child—imagining a place in the world that might fit him perfectly with just a few alterations. He looked at himself and wondered how exactly one might make alterations to an oversize, ill-fitting world.

Was he taking too long, standing there silently? The young man with the CJ teeth looked uncomfortable with the waiting. But Arthur often had problems with time. There were minutes that stretched on like bridges, while whole days swept by like water underneath.

At the end of infinite rows of dark wool shoulders, he was positioned in front of the store's floor-length mirror. He may have been a child but he could become anyone in that coat. "Would you like some coffee, tea?" the Jewish man asked. "Have a seat over there and let's talk coats." Arthur sat, and the coffee was canned and stale.

"I wore a coat once," Arthur told his cellmate, "that was two thousand dollars and I once counted two thousand sausages in the window of a sausage store. Now I've met a man with two-thousand-dollar teeth."

"The fuck you saying?"

Arthur wondered if he'd just lost his chance to try out those teeth. He was about to ask again when the new hippie-looking guy in the top bunk near the door sat up. "What time is it?" he asked.

"About breakfast," Arthur said.

"Well, that's pretty early. Your talking's not very considerate, now is it?"

"You're gay, aren't you?" Arthur said. "You have the coolest look—carnival, I think, with your shaggy hair and beard. You look like you just got shot out of a cannon.

You should see yourself. I wish I looked like you, but with this guy's teeth."

"Thanks, you fucking weirdo."

"You're welcome," said Arthur. "Hey, do you want to act like we're humping next time the guard comes around?"

"It's a little too early for fun and games, isn't it?" The man rubbed the callused tip of his thumb with his index finger. Arthur could smell the remnants of butane and cocaine issue from the friction. "Are you gay too?"

"I wish," said Arthur. "You must dream of going to prison someday."

"No, I don't think I dream of prison."

"You should," Arthur said, not knowing exactly why. He could feel his thoughts slowing now, about to give way to those not his own. If he could just last until after breakfast, they'd walk him down the hall and the nurse would be there, the meds would come and the world would spin faster again, so his own voice could outrun the others.

Four meals came in heavy plastic trays. Arthur gave his eggs to the young man with the expensive teeth. The fourth man slept through the meal, and his food was divided by the two men on the top bunks. They all ate, then lay back down. Arthur lay down with his cape and looked at the underside of the bunk above him. Some of the faded splotches of dried toothpaste still held pictures: glossy school photos of boys and girls, magazine clippings of airbrushed models. There was a pencil sketch of an old wooden cross, a crayon drawing of SpongeBob SquarePants, nude sketches of busty women, a neatly drawn calendar from some July with half its days crossed off.

Arthur had the little tube of toothpaste given to every inmate, but no teeth. He had nothing to paste to the underside of the bunk either. He closed his eyes and was calculating how much toothpaste it would take to attach his body to the underside when a tall deputy with a goatee opened the door.

"Hey, Superman, you gotta see the psych," the deputy said, twirling keys around his finger.

"I need to wait for the nurse."

"Today you see the psych first. Leave the blanket here."

Arthur sat in a room made of yellow cinder blocks with one wall of yellow iron bars. There was a long table in the center and a green chalkboard on the wall. It was the Bible study room, Arthur could tell from the faint, erased chalk words ghosted on the board: *Be patient; establish your hearts, for the coming of the Lord draweth nigh.* Arthur closed his eyes. He felt good and warm there with the remnants of those words.

Doctor Stan, the psychologist, was always in a hurry and Monday was the busiest with all the weekend influx. To make matters worse, his pretty young intern, Jill, was halfway through a pregnancy. Her body was swollen, she wore no makeup, and there was a large, swollen pimple about to burst between her eyes. Doctor Stan seemed her exact opposite—pale and rail-thin, with a patchy beard that made him look sickly, as if he lacked nutrients or something essential.

"So you know why you're here?" Doctor Stan said.

"Yes."

"Can you tell me why you're here?"

"I'd like to order a lobotomy, please."

Doctor Stan and Jill exchanged glances.

"Why do you think you want a lobotomy?"

"I don't know," said Arthur. "I think it'd be nice to have only half a brain. I'd really have an excuse then. I could say something stupid and people would say, 'Figures,' or I could just hang a little chalkboard around my neck—*I have half a brain.* Though it's probably not half, maybe a tenth they take out. They'd just have to get the right part, the part that's gone wrong. But you're the one who'd know about that—you're the professional."

"I don't know anything about lobotomies, actually."

"Well, regardless. I'd like it out. You probably don't understand the perils of a torturous brain."

"Is that an insult?" asked Doctor Stan.

"Is it?" Arthur asked Jill, who shrugged.

"Don't direct your questions to her, and don't answer my questions with a question of your own. I'm here to look out for your safety. And frankly, your attitude smacks of suicidal tendencies. We can put you on C-Wing, you know. But I've heard you're a sleeper, so I doubt you'd like that."

"Doctor Stan, I'm not going to kill myself. But I am tired. So if we're done—"

"Today is different, Arthur. They're going to come and get you for your video arraignment. I'm here to assess your mental state for the proceedings, so you need to answer my questions. Again, do you know why you're here?"

"Because of what I did."

"That's good. That's pretty much all I need. We'll talk more later, Arthur. Maybe."

Doctor Stan nodded to the deputy, and the deputy then swung the steel door open with a loud squeak from its hinges. Arthur walked out, stood against the wall, and waited as the door shut, locking the two clinicians in.

He was left in a small room with the deputy where a table held a color television set with a miniature camera on top. There was a fax machine on another table behind him. On the TV screen was a live shot of a desk and empty chair, a Michigan and an American flag, another desk with another fax machine, a neat stack of bright white paper.

Arthur stared at the empty office for so long he was actually surprised when the judge walked in, robed in black. He sat in his leather chair and tapped the microphone. "Can you hear me?" he asked. He wore half-lensed spectacles and his hair was white and short. His assistant entered and sat at the fax machine. "Can you hear me?" he repeated.

"I can hear you," Arthur said. "You're coming in loud and clear. Bravo, X-ray, marshmallow. Romeo Romeo wherefore tango." There was no end to the words he could hear himself saying—like rabbits from a hat. "Alpha, bravo, calypso, sangria, doctor, doctor, yellow, night-light."

The judge's assistant fed a piece of paper into the fax machine, and the machine behind Arthur began to beep and spit out the same piece of paper at him. The closed-circuit television, the real-time fax relay, the hum of the paper rolling from the machine—it made him feel as if he was being executed by lethal injection. He closed his eyes and imagined the warmth of the serum surging through his body. So calm, so nice, it was hard to care that you were about to die.

His uncle Jimmy Ray had died that way. In Texas, right? No, Kansas. He had uncles in prison all over the country. It might have been Stateville, Illinois—regardless, he had gone with his mother. She could barely walk, and there were no chairs in the witness room, only the window. His uncle looked tiny in the brightly lit room. His arms were strapped to the sickly green gurney. A microphone hung from the ceiling and a red phone stuck to the wall. Jimmy said, "I'm real sorry for all the pain I caused." Arthur's mother cried. Between sobs she kept saying, "He was so good. He was so good." She may have been talking about Jimmy, or she may have meant her other brother that Jimmy had killed.

There was a hum and Jimmy's eyes closed halfway.

"It's working," he said. His eyes closed after another hum and the man pushing the buttons sent one last hum that made his chest stop rising and falling. A doctor came into the room, placed the metal disk of his stethoscope under Uncle Jimmy's shirt, and nodded.

Later, the two of them walked outside in the cool night. His mom smoked Salems. They walked into a gymnasium where, on a table under a basketball hoop, his uncle lay white and still in a long cardboard box. Jimmy wore a white T-shirt and there was a blanket pulled up to his chest. The box was as rigid as plywood and smelled like a new appliance. No one had money to bury Jimmy in a regular cemetery—he'd have an *X* on the white cross, state shorthand for "executed."

The humming motor from the fax machine behind Arthur clicked off. The deputy slid a piece of paper onto the table in front of him. On television, the judge took off his glasses and slipped a curved earpiece into the corner of his mouth. "Do you understand that these are serious charges before you?"

"I do."

"Do you understand that these charges carry a mandatory sentence of life in prison?"

"I do."

Arthur felt like a bride. This was his courthouse wedding, to the state of Michigan, till death do you part. Only then did he truly realize he was on camera—that he was being broadcast to thousands, and that he was the star of this drama unfolding. He signed the list of the charges and the deputy faxed it back to the court, and the paper rolled out of the televised fax machine. It was all happening just as scripted—the beginning and the middle and the end—all of it. It only had to be lived through to be recorded.

"I'm going to order a competency hearing for the defendant and enter a not guilty plea at this time. That's all for today." The judge began to rise.

"Your Honor?"

"Yes?"

"No gavel?"

"Excuse me?"

"You're not going to bang your gavel?"

The judge didn't answer. Arthur watched him rise and soon he was gone. His assistant entered information on a laptop computer and Arthur imagined the credits rolling over her, the theme song playing. The deputy escorted Arthur out of the room and into the elevator.

"What time is it?" Arthur asked, exhausted.

"Ten-thirty."

"Feels like forever."

"Just another day in the KCJ," said the deputy. They rode the elevator to the third floor, and the dark hallway was quiet. They arrived at Arthur's cell.

"Thank you."

"Sure," the deputy said, unlocking the door.

The television was on, loud. The shaft of light that earlier lit a corner now illuminated his bottom bunk. Arthur's picture was on the TV screen above the words

BREAKING NEWS. The man with the golden teeth looked at the screen, then at Arthur, then yelled to the next cell over: "Hey, Marcus, we got a celebrity over here! No shit, that whack job we got is on the TV." Now, all three of the men in the cell looked at Arthur.

Arthur knew what they wanted: for him to take his blanket and tie the corners in front of his throat. And when the newsbreak was over, and that powerful, heroic music erupted from the tiny television speaker, Arthur would stand, step to the top of the steel picnic table, wrap his cape around him with a dramatic sweep, and wait for the drama to unfold. This is what they expect. This is what they need. And who was he to disappoint?

THE BOY WHO DREAMED TOO MUCH

It rained the day six of us rode to quarantine from the county jail in Kalamazoo. I remember because I knew I would want to write about the trip someday, and I was sure the rain would sound like a prop—something to foreshadow the darkness of prison. But it isn't—it just rained. If there was anything that could serve as a prop, it was the windows. The windows of the van were completely fogged over, effectively erasing us—we were there, but we weren't.

I was cuffed by my right hand to Ray, my cellmate in County for the past five months. He was in his mid-fifties, a short, stocky man who paid too much attention to his hair and harbored enough hatred for his ex-stepdaughter for me to think there was something seriously wrong with him. After being in the same room with the man for so long, seeing him prance around the cell in nothing but boxers, constantly slicking his hair back with cold water, I had hoped prison would bring some relief from him. Yet there I was, closer than ever.

In all fairness to Ray, he probably would have liked to be free from me too. We used the hour-long ride to Jackson, Michigan, to dream aloud about the perks of quarantine over jail—what it would be like to go outside every day, to smoke and drink coffee, as that's all we knew about quarantine, besides that it was the one to two months between County and prison where we would be evaluated extensively (medically and mentally) to determine which of Michigan's forty-plus prisons (and Level 1, 2, or 4) we would be sent to. We would have a single cell and a little more freedom than we'd previously had, and we all looked forward to Jackson as if it were a tropical island resort.

Micky was in the van with us, in the backseat talking about his dreams with the guy he was cuffed to. I only heard bits and pieces: "Listen to this one," or "What do you think a dream like that means?" I wanted to tell him something I had heard in a song once: no one wants to hear about another's dream unless the listener is in it. But I didn't. I figured he was probably nervous, like all of us, and he dealt with it by talking.

We couldn't see out the van's windows, so we got our first view of prison when we stepped out into the rain and even then all we could see was a half mile of concrete wall with one white metal guard tower at each end. The enormity of the wall was enough to shut us all up. We were a chatty group before, but now each of us stayed quiet, looking down the length of what seemed to be the rest of our lives.

We stood in the rain as the deputies checked in their weapons and signed paperwork. Everyone just looked around, at the wall, or down at our orange flip-flops. Tommy, a young meth cooker, squinted and grimaced as if he had to take a shit. We had spent an hour together in the County's holding cell waiting to leave, so I knew he had twenty-five Seroquel stuck up his rectum. He was struggling to keep the drugs in place. Through the handcuff I could feel Ray's hand shaking, or maybe it was mine.

"This doesn't look much better than County," Ray said.

Micky overheard and walked up next to him. His cuff partner was a frizzy-headed kid with an ever-present smile. We all called him Sideshow. "Ah, don't worry too much, old school," said Micky. "You can't tell what's inside from what's outside."

"That's true," I said, and the group of us followed the deputies through a fence that slowly rolled back to let us pass. We walked along a wide sidewalk with another pair of high fences on either side, and signs posted every twenty feet that read: VOLTAGE.

"Hey, Wiggins," Micky said to one of the deputies. "What kind of voltage you think is running through that fence?"

"Why don't you grab it and find out?" Wiggins said.

"All right," Micky said, and pulled Sideshow toward

the fence. Sideshow just smiled, apparently not realizing the current would pass through the handcuffs into him too.

Wiggins turned around, smiling until he saw Micky reaching. The smile dropped and his eyes went black—he must have seen his twenty years of service washed away in lawyers and television crews, microphones and a face-to-face with the mayor of Kalamazoo.

Micky's hand got a couple of inches away before he pulled it back. Wiggins had taken two steps in his direction. His partner went after him and was ready to step between, but they were eye to eye when Wiggins whispered something under his breath and walked away.

"What do you think he said?" Ray asked me as we neared the entrance to the processing center.

Micky piped up. "He wished me long life, good health, and sweet dreams at night." He and Sideshow entered the building. The electric door shushed closed behind them.

Ray was legally deaf without his hearing aids, which he hadn't seen since the night he was arrested for shooting his estranged wife dead. "What did he say?" he asked.

"He wished him a good life and sweet dreams."

"Really? That's pretty nice."

"Yeah," I said. The electric door slid open, we walked in, and Ray began to whistle softly. I didn't have the heart to quiet him.

We were taken to a room with sheets of white paper covering half the floor in random squares. We were uncuffed and told to strip. The deputies collected the County jumpsuits, flip-flops, and handcuffs and left without a word. There was one guard there, small and bald. One of the guys asked if we were to strip completely.

"If your old lady asked you to strip would you stand around asking if she meant completely?"

We took off our socks and underwear too. We put on faded blue, ill-fitting prison jumpsuits and filled out the medical forms that lay scattered on the floor of the room. Pictures were taken and tattoos were listed for our ID cards. Fingerprints were scanned into a computer. In a small, private room I told a lady the names of my next of kin before she injected me with a TB test and hepatitis vaccination.

We showered and went to the gymnasium for our clothes. Fellow inmates stood at tables stenciling on our numbers using rollers and white paint. Months ago, after our convictions or plea deals, we had each been given our six digits, but this was the first time we had seen them on our clothes: three button-up blue shirts; three pairs of pants; five pairs of tube socks; three T-shirts; two thermal shirts; two thermal underpants; five pair of briefs; a canvas belt; a bright orange sock hat; a blue baseball cap; a blue and orange winter coat; black dress shoes; white tennis shoes; and two pairs of pajamas. A small paper bag held five metered envelopes, a flexible pen, and fifty pages of writing paper. We took turns changing clothes in the wide-open restroom, dropping our jumpsuits on an ever-rising pile. We each had a heavy, dark green bag to carry it all, and with the orange stripe running down the length of our legs and across our backs, we looked like a bowling team in brand-new outfits as we walked out of the gym. Micky and I stopped near each other. "Shoes," he said.

"Yeah," I said, and we looked at our feet as if we had a couple of fish there. Neither of us had worn shoes in a very long time. They felt like an old, favorite song.

A guard told us simply, "Library." Micky and I hesitated because we didn't know the way, and he called us a couple of dumb motherfuckers. I knew that he too would seem like a prop if I described his big, fat, miserable face and his stellar vocabulary, but there you go.

In the library, we sat at long tables with other new and returning prisoners. We were handed plastic bags with peanut butter and jelly sandwiches, juice, and potato chips. A middle-aged man sporting a mustache and calling himself Z gave us information on AIDS and explained how tattoos in prison were the most common way to contract HIV. "But sex is a big spreader too," he said, and laughed.

"What do you do if someone wants to give you a pack of cigarettes for free?" Z asked.

A small black man in the front row answered: "You don't take it."

"And why not?" Z reached into his front pocket, slipped out a Pall Mall, and tossed it to the man.

"Because he'll want to get paid."

Z asked a few more questions, rewarding the men who answered with cigarettes. He told us we could trade our metered envelopes for four cigarettes to the other prisoners who were in quarantine awhile, but some would try to give us three. He said that our objective was to make it through the next five or six weeks and "be on the next bus rolling" to our destination prison. Z seemed nice enough, which is what made the whole experience more frightening—one person of authority would be a decent example of humanity and the next would be a raging numbskull. It was like living with manic, dysfunctional parents—warm and accepting one minute, cold and abusive the next.

Z wished our group luck. We shouldered our duffel bags and walked out into the large recreation yard behind the prison walls. The rain had softened to a light, foggy drizzle. Guys were huddled in groups of five or six smoking the new cigarettes. The smoke surrounded them in a soft blue haze that lifted slowly into the air. I hadn't smoked in nearly eleven months and that sweet, earthy smell of burning tobacco caused me to think of home and all the pain I'd caused. I thought of my children and freedom, everything I'd taken and lost. Tommy, the guy with the kiestered Seroquel, was sharing a cigarette with Micky. He saw me watching and motioned me over. He offered me the cigarette and saw my hand shake as I reached for it. "I know, I'm shaking too," he said. He noticed the water in my eyes and looked across the yard.

It's a phenomenon between prisoners in the presence of another's emotions—they look away and become quiet. It's one boundary we all respect.

I took a slow drag off Tommy's hand-rolled and instantly became light-headed. I had imagined that moment for a long time, and though I always assumed I would cough, I didn't. Micky took a drag and asked Tommy where he got it. "One of the guys where we got our clothes traded some for an envelope," he said. "Is this the first time down for both of you?" Micky and I nodded.

"Just be careful who you hang around with, don't mess with anyone's sissy, don't gamble, and you'll be fine. Prison ain't like it used to be. What about him?" he said, nodding toward Ray, who was still whistling as he stared out into the yard at nothing in particular. "It's gonna be rough for him."

Tommy didn't give a reason but he didn't have to. We knew.

There were four guards outside with us waiting for lists telling where we were to be housed. Tommy lit another cigarette and blew a smoke ring that just skimmed the top of Micky's shaved head. "I dreamed about all this years ago," Micky said. He was looking toward the continuous line of brick buildings across the yard. "Is that where we're going?"

"I'm not sure how they do things now," said Tommy, handing the cigarette to me. "You may start out in the South Buildings, or you may start out in Seven Block.

I heard now if you're a violent, they start you in Seven. What'd you do?"

Micky looked at the ground. "Robbed a bank," he said. I could tell he didn't want to talk about it, and I thought Tommy would respect that, but he didn't. He wanted to find out if Micky was lying, if he was a molester trying to cover it up. "How'd you get caught?"

"My mom," he said.

"How'd she know?"

"She found my disguise."

"What was it?"

"A clown."

"No shit," said Tommy. "That was you?"

Micky looked up and smiled like a C-list celebrity happy to be recognized. "I had the hair, the nose, the clothes—I had everything but the big shoes. I could never find a pair of big shoes." Micky had a pronounced forehead that overshadowed his eyes. He had jutting cheekbones, acne around his temples, and scraggly hair on his chin. There was a half-finished homemade tattoo heart on his forearm, probably made in County with a diabetic lancet.

"You were probably better off without those shoes," Tommy said, tossing the cigarette butt to the sidewalk. "No way you could have run in them."

"No, you don't understand," said Micky. "They would have been lucky. I could fly with the shoes in my dream. I think that means I would have never gotten caught. But hey, so, is bank robbery a violent crime?"

"Yeah," Tommy said.

"I kind of figured."

"Did it ever occur to you to not rob a bank in a getup like that? That just because you dreamed it—"

"No," Micky said. "It was perfect. I don't regret a thing except the shoes."

"Well fucking A, then. So were you a happy clown, or a sad clown?"

"Oh, sad, definitely—it was serious business."

I watched Tommy as he took in this last answer. I had known a guy in County who knew exactly what I was thinking in times like these. I always figured he could read it on my face, and as I looked at Tommy smiling, I knew he wasn't imagining at all what I was: I could think only of this poor kid's tennis shoes—dirty, worn-out, sadder than any makeup he could ever paint on his face.

Tommy summed things up: "In here there are far worse things you could be than a fucked-up clown. Yup, there are worse things."

The guards got their prisoner lists and split us into two groups. The six of us from Kalamazoo were split in half with Micky, Ray, and me on one side. We thanked Tommy for the smoke and he wished us well, "God-speed," I think he said. Maybe "God bless." God was in there, whatever it was.

We passed through the new hospital annex and entered a different part of the prison property. The large buildings we had seen were now to our backs, and joined another long row that was only a vague shape within the mist in the distance. We walked along the razor-wire fence encircling the prison's yard. At our side was a quarter mile of open field, but it was misty enough that I couldn't see the end of that either. As if on cue, we began to hear voices off to our right, catcalls for the new arrivals. Micky and I and some of the others laughed, but Ray and a few more veered away from the fence.

Micky spit, then yelled. "I'll climb that fence and fuck you up, bitch!"

The fifty or so men who had by now crossed the running track let out a collective "Oooh," and laughed. There was a regulation-size football field marked off with bright orange pylons and a game in progress. Past the football field was one, maybe two baseball fields, and everything beyond that the mist hid from sight.

Ray walked up beside me. "I thought prison wasn't like that anymore. I didn't think people got raped anymore," he said.

"Those guys were just messing around."

"Well, it's not funny."

"Yeah, well, you may as well laugh."

He spoke slowly then, trying to share what I imagine was something like disappointment: "I thought things would make more sense once we got here, at least more than County, but nothing seems to. Do you know what I mean?"

"You'll be fine, Ray," I said.

We had moved out of range from the catcalling. The

full duffel bag was getting heavier in my hand. Some men had the bags across their shoulders. We walked through what could have been an abandoned industrial complex—empty warehouses and uninhabited cellblocks. There were bars on all the windows and small video cameras mounted high in the corners of the buildings. A water tower overshadowed an empty basketball court, and a chapel with a tall bell stood unused. We passed several empty greenhouses and then began to see signs of life—the grass was manicured and trash cans were freshly painted. There was an apple tree, pigeons pecking at fallen fruit. Through a window in a two-story building I saw a very bright light. I stopped to look and to shift the duffel bag to my shoulder.

I could see shelving with new plants under bright growing lights. Some of them were bushy and long, their leafy vines cascading to the shelf below. It looked like a jungle awash in Amazon sunlight and I imagined working around all those lights, snipping leaves and caring for the plants in the soft, black, jungle dirt. We kept walking but I kept looking back, trying to capture another flash of that light, before it was lost to the mist.

We came to the wide, steel doors and a sign above neatly painted in red script: 7 BLOCK. 7 Block was like all the other cellblocks we had passed, except it was inhabited. Upon reaching our destination I realized neither the guards, the razor wire, nor the walls held us in place. It was the confusion. By the time we reached 7 Block, I had no idea which way was out.

We entered the building and heard the steady hum of five hundred men talking. We walked down the center of five stories of single-man cells. Prisoners on the ground level tried to trade us cigarettes for envelopes, but with a guard in front and one at our backs, none of us stopped. We sat at tables near the end of the cellblock and a woman with a bullhorn called us up to the third-floor officer's station one at a time to get our cell assignments and two nylon netted laundry bags. The tags on mine read: 35-3-7, for Cell 35, third level, 7 Block. Micky was Cell 34 on the second level, and Ray was cell 12 on my level.

I waited in front of my cell for the door to open. I was met by a young black man who introduced himself as Popcorn and asked if I wanted to trade some envelopes for cigarettes.

"Yeah," I said, and dug three out of my duffel bag. He handed me twelve neatly rolled smokes and a pack of matches. His hands had been badly burned and the tendons stuck out in relief from under the scar tissue. I wondered if the burn had something to do with his nickname, but I didn't ask.

My cell door opened and I went in. There were bars at the back as well with a walkway behind them. I could hear Micky talking to his new neighbors in his cell below mine. I put a sheet on the sickly green mattress, sat on the end, and looked across the space to the cells on the other side. Men were living their lives—reading paperback novels and Bibles, writing letters, napping, combing their hair, brushing teeth, exercising, a Muslim faced east on the floor. I wondered how he knew which way east was.

"How can you tell when it's safe to smoke?" I asked Popcorn.

"You can't tell from the back—you get caught, you get caught. From the front, though, get someone's attention on the other side and they'll look out."

So I whistled shyly and got no one's attention. "You got to do it like this," Popcorn said, and whistled loudly. A guy in a T-shirt and pajama bottoms on the second level looked up. I waved my cigarette at him; he looked left, then right, and gave me the thumbs-up.

I lit the cigarette. The match hissed out in the stainless-steel toilet and I blew smoke toward the back of the cell while watching the man on the second level. I smoked half, knocked the ember off into the toilet bowl, and flushed. The flush sounded like a jet at takeoff, and I could feel air sucking down with the water. I lay down on the bed, went to sleep, and dreamed that someone kept stealing the batteries from the radio I once owned as a kid.

The next morning, Micky, Ray, and I were called out early to have our TB tests read. On the way back I looked up at that brightly lit indoor jungle without mentioning it to Ray or Micky. Another fence rolled back and we walked up to a guard who checked our yellow call-out sheets against our IDs. Micky talked about his dream last night the whole way. "I was driving a Ferrari, right? But it wasn't on a road, it was through a shopping mall filled with Halloween costumes."

We were passing the open yard where the catcalls had been hurled the day before. Razor wire ran over the top of the fence and along the ground in front. Men jogged around the track, and nearer to the five-story cellblocks, they lifted weights. It could have been a college campus. There was probably half a mile of distance between us and the hospital building. That much space gave me the feeling I always got while looking at oceans, or across some huge square in Moscow or Venice, though I'd never been to either. The sight caused me to long vaguely for those places—a false nostalgia made from space and mist.

"But the shifter is all backwards," said Micky, "so I can't figure out how to make the car go fast at all. And this hot bitch is in the front seat with me—turns out, it's the mom from that show, *The Sopranos,* but we start fighting because her husband is chasing us. Finally we end up doing it in a New Jersey hardware store. So, what do you think?" We were approaching the hospital annex.

"I think you've got mother issues," I said.

"What? It wasn't *my* mom. It's the hot chick from TV."

"Still," I said. "Did you and your mom get along?"

"Hell no. She turned me in, the bitch."

"I know, but before that."

"I gave her crack when she wanted it," he said. "Fuck

it, man, never mind." We walked into the hospital and stood in a long line to have a nurse check if the injection site was swollen. We were all clean.

We took our time walking back, smoking and looking around. The mist had lifted somewhat and we could see the end of the field opposite the large prison yard. There were the two guard towers perched atop a long gray wall. The windows of the towers were darkly tinted. Why, I wondered, did they not want us to see in?

"They're having a huge hurricane down in Louisiana," Ray said. "The guy in line behind me gets the paper. He said it'll be raining up here by Sunday." He looked up at the sky, which was as gray as it was on the ground. Micky and I kept walking, but Ray stopped and began to cry. His shoulders shook and saliva flew out of his mouth when he coughed. He took off his glasses and buried his face in his hands. "I can't fucking take this," he said. "I can't take any of this. All my life I just walked in the woods, just walked in the woods . . ." His words trailed off into more sobs. I put my hand on his shoulder and Micky stood apart, watching. We had heard the "walked in the woods" speech before—it was when he was happy, alone and happy, before he met his estranged wife. What more could we say to cheer him up that we hadn't already tried to say in County: that people make mistakes; you can't look back; there is a reason for everything; life's a bitch sometimes. Ray straightened up and began to walk again, slowly, like a man who'd had the wind kicked from him. The truth was, I envied his ability to break down and let the pain loose. "Whew," he said. "Sorry."

Micky and I walked on either side of Ray as if he were physically injured and his knees might buckle any second.

"There's good news," Micky said.

"Yeah?" said Ray.

"You're TB free."

"Who says I want to be? I wish I had something terminal." This seemed to lift Ray's spirits because he chuckled slightly. I knew what he was experiencing—the first time when you realize you are not afraid to die, that in fact, you welcome it. It had dawned on me one night in County when I couldn't sleep because my stomach hurt, but only on one side. I came to the conclusion that my liver was finally failing after twenty years of drinking. This thought wasn't a minute old when it hit me as clearly as if someone in the room had spoken: *I hope it's shot to hell.* Then I fell asleep calmly, imagining the peace that would come from not having to face the future I had ahead of me.

"As a matter of fact," Ray said, "I wish they had the death penalty in Michigan. Ha!"

I watched Ray as this new realization settled on him. He had a crooked grin and a calm, satisfied look in his eyes. There was an aura of freedom about him, realizing that in his new life, death was now a fantasy.

There was no grass to speak of in the "yard" at 7 Block, yet that's what the officer called it over the bullhorn at 8:00 a.m., when our doors broke open. Ah, yard, I thought: grass, the apple tree, walks on wood-chipped paths. My mind was not yet turned to the Prison Channel.

About two hundred men were herded past the chow hall to a large, fenced-in basketball court catty-cornered from my secret jungle room. We were shaded by another cellblock and it was cold with the late August chill. I had the feeling we were in a dimly lit cooler. Ray, Micky, and I walked in a circle around the border of the basketball court. Ten men played ball, pausing to blow through their cold fingers every chance they got. "So this is yard," Ray said.

"Kind of pisses a guy off, don't it?" said Micky. Groups of men sat at the picnic tables playing cards. Popcorn was weaving another man's hair into cornrows. Micky put his gloves and bright orange hat on. "I had this dream last night," he began.

"Hey, Micky—guess what?" Ray said.

"What?"

"No one wants to hear about your fucking dreams. Who ever told you they did?"

"But this is a good one, Ray."

"Unless you can tell the future with them and I'm out walking free, I don't want to hear any more of that shit."

"Or what?" he said. "What are you going to do, Ray? You don't have a gun and I ain't your defenseless wife. You're fucked, Ray. You're fucked, so you might as well listen."

Micky waited for a moment, hopping up and down

slightly to keep warm. When Ray didn't say anything, Micky resumed with his dream. "We're in a museum, or it might have been a school, but anyway, there are these paintings on the wall, but they're not regular paintings, I mean, they look like it, but they are set up with mirrors and this naked girl shows me how you can stick your hand through them to, like, another dimension. Then we left and there are all these burned trees and houses around with bombs and mushroom clouds in the distance, but she's just cartwheeling through it all. Cartwheeling and dancing, until I grab her around the neck and start choking her. Then I woke up. What do you think about that?"

"I think some girl really did a number on you, Micky," I said. "I think you hate women."

"Yup," said Ray. "And that hurricane's coming."

We looked up into the cold, blue sky for a coming apocalypse.

"I don't hate women," Micky said. "And that hurricane won't be a hurricane by the time it gets to Michigan. Besides, it's got nothing to do with my dream."

"It may not be a hurricane when it gets here, but you never know what it'll bring," Ray said. "Once I was backpacking up the Cumberland Trail in Virginia, when a hurricane came up the coast and—"

"This isn't Virginia, dumb-ass," said Micky.

"No, it's not. I'm just saying."

"You're an idiot, Ray, with your hurricane speech."

"How about both of you just cool it," I said. We

stopped walking and stood by a row of telephones. Lines of men two and three deep stood waiting to talk. The three of us had turned in our phone lists, which had to be checked by the DOC and then sent to the phone company, a process that would take a month, at least. Men talked to their wives, girlfriends, and children. The ten guys played basketball. I don't think they were keeping score, but they seemed to be having fun. The sun began to slip over the top of the cellblock and a line of light moved toward the row of phones—an imperceptible movement, unless you tracked its position against a rock or small hole in the ground. I stayed there and watched the line of sunlight as it swept the yard, turning the fragile frost it touched into a tiny wisp of steam.

We didn't see the sun for a very long time after that cool August Saturday. The rain hurled up at us from Hurricane Katrina; we could hear it outside during church the next morning. A thin, old Baptist preacher reminded us that we were all God's children. The fifty or so of us were excellent, angelic singers since the acoustics of 7 Block are similar to a bathroom or cathedral. Even the men who didn't go to the services stood in the fronts of their cells, applauding after each song. That Sunday was so dark that many cells had their ceiling lights on, and as the men stood in their lit rooms listening, it could have passed for the world's largest stained-glass installation, a vast, colorful window of humanity.

After church I ordered what I could from the commissary with the five dollars that had followed me from County—a pouch of Bugler tobacco, twelve generic instant coffee packages, and a twenty-two-ounce plastic cup. I mixed a cup of lukewarm coffee and began rolling cigarettes. The small piles of shredded tobacco were still damp and smelled like sweet, wet grass. Thunder from outside boomed and echoed throughout the block. I gave a couple freshly rolled cigarettes to the prison porters who were always passing with their brooms and cleaning supplies. I felt free that Sunday, rolling smokes and drinking coffee. For a while I was in a Manhattan bookstore on the corner of Prince and Mulberry, sunk in a seat by the window and looking up every once in a while to watch the pretty people pass. Then I was on the Oregon coast watching the tide slip out under high, white cliffs while someone's dog fetched a stick through the salty foam. I raced through early morning Kalamazoo to the hospital, missing my son's premature birth once again by two minutes. I ate deep-fried whole fish on Cozumel, then signed up for scuba lessons and swam among the coral and neon fish so bright they seemed fake. I thought about a tall, chubby kid in County who said he was going to wear his blanket as a cape into the courtroom and demand that the judge refer to him as King Arthur. I wondered if he ever did.

I spent the first Sunday in quarantine in dreams of

my own, the first freedom I'd known in nearly a year. Despite the caffeine, I fell asleep shortly after the lights went out at ten.

I woke up early on Monday and found a yellow call-out sheet between the bars. "Psychological Testing, Zone 1." By then we had all heard about the test: a five-hour marathon with over five hundred questions, one of which was going to be "Have you ever wanted to be a woman?" I had been toying with the idea of answering all of the questions with absolute honesty. Every man, at one time or another, has thought of what being female might feel like. I figured I could honestly answer "Yes."

After breakfast ten of us began the walk to Zone 1, Micky and Ray included. The weather was colder and thick with a fog that seemed to cling to the edges of things, softening and swallowing them at fifty feet or so. There were patches in the asphalt that had worn away to the previous brick surface and the red, clay-colored brick was slick with dew. A light breeze blew the fog around like sheer, white curtains.

I looked for my jungle room, but couldn't find it. Ray came up beside me. "What's up with Micky?" he said.

"What do you mean?"

"He's quiet. He's not talking at all. I feel kind of bad."

"I thought you wanted him to be quiet." I was lagging, trying to figure out if I was looking up at the wrong building. Eventually I gave up. Ray and I walked quickly to catch up with Micky as we neared the gate.

"What were you looking for back there?" Ray asked.

"Nothing," I said. "Hey, Micky, did you dream about the big test we have to take today?"

"Nah." He smiled. We came to that part of the path with the vast, open prison yard to our left and the open field to our right. I couldn't see any building structures at all. Micky stopped, and the other men walked past, talking about questions on the test and all their smart-ass answers. Micky stepped off the path and into the thick, brown grass. He looked at me.

"Did you have a dream last night, Micky?"

"Yeah I did. But you're right, Ray, I talk about my dreams too much."

"I'm not right, Micky. No, I'm not. No, I'm not."

Micky turned around to walk through the damp field, stepping high so he wouldn't soak his feet, which made little sense given what he was doing. He was swallowed by the fog before he even got close to the off-limits sign. He reappeared just once, the blue of his uniform softer now in the distant white curtains. Soon, he was gone for good. I kept looking, knowing he was there, but I never saw him again.

"They're going to shoot him," Ray said.

"Maybe not," I said. "Maybe they'll—"

And we heard it: the single crack and the faint echoes fading through the dense, wet air. Before the sound had finished, Ray and I instinctively dropped facefirst to the pavement. He began to cry and I didn't care. The thought occurred to me to persuade Ray to follow Micky's path—Ray was so goddamn annoying, I wanted to kill him myself at times, and he was needy and dumb enough to follow almost any suggestion. But I didn't try.

The deafening whine of the lockdown siren began, and I thought of the future.

Do they shoot you in the head, or go for a wound?

What would keep me from walking toward the wall someday?

All people are stories and I wish I knew for sure about Micky. I wish the veil of fog had lifted and I could have seen his story end clearly. I wish the ending wasn't only the beginning.

573543

Goodbye to the river and to Jonnie Rae, whom I don't remember. The river is real—as real as the cell I'm in now—with a name, the Kalamazoo. I rented an apartment near that river in a town of the same name. That much is real, I know for sure.

I was working as a meat-casing salesman. Not the old-fashioned hog intestines or newer collagen casings for sausage—but high-tech, trilayered plastics that secreted different flavors and colors of smoke to the oblong slabs of turkey and ham that millions eat every day in delis across the country. I would fly out of Gerald R. Ford in Grand Rapids, work the Chicago area one week, then to Philadelphia the next.

Most of my time was spent running tests in large processing plants—tagging our sample casings after they'd been stuffed full of sticky ham or turkey emulsion. When you think of a turkey sandwich, you're really thinking of turkey emulsion—a nearly liquid, perfectly consistent batter made by running ground meat through what is basically a home blender times one thousand. I measured shrinkage after cooking and monitored the purge levels, or water loss. On the business end, lost water equals lost weight equals lost profit. My job was to find the perfect liquid smoke additive that could balance the pH, make the casing peel properly, and give the end product the perfect outer color and flavor. It was a white whale in a brown bottle, and there was a lot of failure, of course. But when it all came together, I'd find myself in a Fortune 500 test kitchen passing around warm hunks of lunch meat to a dozen executives, and success tasted just like a late-night raid on a leftover Christmas ham.

It was a rewarding, well-paying job, but I was on my own a lot of the time, and strange things happen to an addict left alone too much. So much of the job involved sitting on planes, and eight years of sobriety slipped imperceptibly away with the muscle relaxers I took to relieve the strain on my back. I told myself the relaxers were okay—I wasn't taking them to get high, after all. But little by little, like stars coming on at night, the distant fires returned. Soon, I would find myself looking up at the cold night sky without realizing the dark had come.

It was a few months of doctor-prescribed Soma, Flexeril, and Skelaxin before I discovered easier ways of getting drugs on the Internet—websites and forums set up by chronic pain sufferers sharing information and resources. Drugshare.com is where I first heard of ketamine, a painkilling pet anesthetic.

To a normal person, a pet anesthetic injected intravenously might sound scary. For me, the appeal was not only analgesic; ketamine was said to produce visions as well. The user basically entered a fifteen-minute coma without any variation in pulse or breath rate. It is used every day in vet offices worldwide and was historically used in wartime for short, painless procedures where opiates are too sedating. It was quick, effective, and just shy of illicit, enough that I could tell myself I wasn't using again.

I found a seller—Joseph from Cebu City, Philippines. Joseph sold a variety of Schedule III drugs: sleeping pills, buprenorphine, muscle relaxers, aspirin with codeine, all manner of benzodiazepines, and a drug called Pharmased—50 mg per ml of pharmaceutical ketamine. Twenty dollars for a 10 ml vial, five vial minimum.

In the Chicago area, I stayed at the Comfort Inn off the 294 Tollway in Harvey, Illinois. At a nearby Mailboxes Etc., I leased six months on a mailbox under the name of Carl Gauss, a nineteenth-century astronomer I'd heard about while tuning my radio. I sent an international money order to Joseph and waited. And waited and waited. E-mails from Joseph told me to be patient, but after two months I was beginning to think I had been taken. All the Drugshare message boards were pro-Joseph, but who knew, all those people may well have been Joseph.

Then, in early September, it came—a discreetly packaged college-level engineering book, *Forms and Functions of the Transitory Square,* Bubble-Wrapped, hollowed-out, filled with cotton and a plastic holder containing five vials of Pharmased. I sat in the strip mall parking lot and held one of the vials in my hand. It seemed magical—cool and light and clear—a potion of possibilities.

I drove down the road a block to the large supermarket. I waited in the car a few minutes wondering if just anyone was allowed to purchase syringes. I had thought about the question before, but never believed I'd get this far: actually walking through the balloon displays at the flower department, past the baby formula, diapers, boxes of cold remedies, antacids, cough medicines, and then to the pharmacy desk with its small, semiprivate window. I stood a courteous three feet behind a man sporting a ridiculously fitted toupee. Viagra, I thought. Now, when I remember him, I think cancer and cringe at the asshole I once was.

The man stepped away, and the pharmacy tech asked how she could help me. "I need some syringes, please." She pulled a clipboard from under the counter and asked what size.

"I don't know," I said.

"So they aren't for you?"

"I have a friend," I said. "I want to make sure he doesn't use dirty needles."

She smiled at me sympathetically. "I'll give you thirty-gauge," she said, handing me the clipboard. "It's so the company can account for the needles." I signed the name Carl Gauss and paid for the syringes, as well as cotton balls and a bottle of rubbing alcohol.

Back at the Comfort Inn I fired up my laptop and got on the Internet, wanting to clean the slate before going on the ride. I answered e-mails concerning future appointments in Philly. I filled out two test reports and e-mailed them to our technical expert. I turned off the computer and cell phone, drew the curtains, and dead-bolted the door. I had read that ketamine users, above any other precaution, should avoid outside disturbances of light or sound. Just enough light glowed around the drawn shades and through the center line of the curtains, and in the dim light I removed the plastic band from the top of the vial, stuck the needle through the small cork opening, and filled the syringe with 0.5 ml. I tapped the air out of the needle and slapped my forearm, just like in the movies. I rested the needle's tip in the center of my arm, but started to shake and pulled it away. I took some deep breaths and tried again, this time anchoring the needle slightly below the skin. I felt the needle tremble in my arm as I pushed it halfway in, and before I thought too much about what I was doing, I sunk the plunger. I pulled it out, swabbed the area with alcohol, and capped the needle. I put the syringe and cotton ball on the nightstand, then lay back on the bed and closed my eyes.

I suppose I should have been preparing myself by focusing on breathing and clearing my mind. But I waited and thought about work—an ongoing project eight hundred miles away at a pork plant north of Philly. It involved a supposedly groundbreaking paper-silicone film developed for whole-muscle hams. It would replace the expensive collagen wrap we currently used, but so far, we had been unable to get it to slide properly through the forming cars of the Tipper Tie assembler. It was basically a paper jam on a massive and incredibly technical scale.

I imagined each step, troubleshooting the process and letting my mind drift, until I became conscious of a slow and steady buzz, like my entire body was humming a song in bass monotone. The hum faded and I felt my body melt away—I was now only a shapeless being of energy, a glow contained in some sort of mechanized casket, sliding through stainless-steel streets between tall, black buildings. I didn't know where I was going, but I knew it was good; I had no needs, no sense of lack. I slid down sharp hills like an amusement park ride and my stomach tingled with the loss of gravity. Near the end, I slowed and entered a cave of complete darkness. A pinprick of light in the distance grew to consume me as the casket dropped away like a shell. I was high up in the light and below me were millions of my fellow beings waiting for me to descend into them.

Then it was over. I opened my eyes. I found my arms folded over my chest, as if I actually had been in a casket all along.

The next evening at the Comfort Inn I closed the curtains, turned off the cell phone and computer, and returned to the vein. It went much smoother this time, as a puff of red colored the clear liquid in the syringe when the needle hit the flow of blood. When I woke, the needle was still there, and the skin had begun to heal around the metal. I had to twist the needle to get it free and apply pressure with a cotton ball. Eventually I learned that's what the belt was for—to keep the drug from hitting long enough to pull the needle out. The movies always make drug use look easy. It actually takes practice.

Some of the prisoners here wear the numbers of the dead. According to the Department of Corrections, the prisoner has been "released by death," and they just reuse the number. My first bunkie, Pepper Pie, had a number like that.

The dead men's numbers were just another odd fact in the strange new world I found myself in. Another I discovered one night as I tried to fall asleep on my bunk. Pepper Pie stood up from the bunk below and walked in his sock feet to the door. He thought I was asleep, I'm sure. If he thought otherwise, he probably would never have done it.

Our cinder-block rooms were the prison standard eight by twelve, with two small desks against the wall opposite the steel-framed bunk beds. One narrow window sat in the center of the solid steel door, which slid open and closed electronically by front desk officers who man a control panel straight out of NASA. Pepper Pie stood in front of the window for a moment, then slowly reached through the thick glass all the way to his elbow, where he seemed unable to go any farther, as if he'd reached the end of an invisible rope, or encountered a barrier I couldn't see. He drew his arm back into the cell, then did the same thing twice more, like reps of a strange exercise. He would get an inch or two farther each time and could reach nearly up to his shoulder. After ten minutes or so, he lay down and slept until lunch the next day.

At night, things like that can happen—mistakes of perception brought on by a softening of the real. I figured I was just seeing things, until a few nights later when he stood up again in the middle of the night. He looked back at me and I closed my eyes before he could see I was awake. He walked to the door again and stood there. He didn't reach through the glass this time. This time, he faded. He faded a few shades short of invisible, as if he was behind a crusty shower curtain, then he came back up to full strength. After that he lay back down and slept until lunch.

Most nights, as far as I knew, he slept. But every third or fourth night, he practiced. With the rest in between, he seemed to grow stronger. After about two months, Pepper Pie could disappear completely for a full sixty-four seconds, and he could push his entire arm, along with half of his shoulder, through the window. As much as I was dying to ask him about it, I figured he wouldn't like me knowing. It was no use, anyway. Why would he tell me anything? What if it was all tied up in the fact that he wore a dead man's number? If that was the case, I was out of luck. My number was permanent. There would never be any hope of losing it for as long as I lived.

I met Jonnie Rae at night too, on the outside. I was standing on the porch of my apartment clapping and stomping to some jazzed-up chamber music coming from the dark law office across Park Street. The building was converted from a Church of Christ, Scientist and had stained-glass windows lit softly from the inside. Jonnie Rae walked by and said, "What are you doing?"

"Enjoying the music," I said.

"You appreciate that sort of thing, do you?"

"I'm sure there are plenty of old people around here who think it's too late, but not me."

"Never too late," Jonnie Rae said. "Well, I'll be seeing you." She continued on down the sidewalk toward town. I went back inside and fastened my new Armani belt around my arm.

Jonnie Rae eventually became my best friend, which, I'll admit, isn't saying much. On nights I was home, he or she would show up and silently listen to music with me. I can't categorize Jonnie Rae's gender—I don't know, and it didn't matter. I realize now that by looking back at her I am trying to make solid what only ever seemed vaporous. She was tall, that's certain. And extremely thin—sometimes when she turned, I could just barely see her in profile. Her hair was different every time we met: up or down, pulled back with dark streaks of moody colors smoldering in certain lights. *Cool* seems like the best descriptor for her, as cool as the air on the nights that I'd see her, and just as fleeting.

Pepper Pie and I talked, of course, but prison talk is generally superficial. Most prisoners have spent their formative years having their trust continually compromised, so to trust another person with information, or emotions, is a sign of weakness. They don't want to seem weak, so they offer up very little. I never learned the full story of why he was here; "I got drunk" is all he would say about it. I knew that he read the Bible for an hour a day, and I knew the only money he had coming in was the fifty-six cents a day he was paid for his laundry-porter job.

I knew why he was called Pepper Pie. In chow hall, some men get impatient with the plastic pepper shakers and instead slam the top into the corner of the table, opening a large, irregular hole. Pepper Pie had grabbed an altered shaker one day, and as a stream of pepper hit his green beans, some flecks spotted his apple pie. On any given day you'll get three or four guys asking if you're going to eat your pie, but that day no one asked him. And since the pepper is cheap, with little or no flavor, he started adding some to his pie daily, "as a bug repellent," he'd say.

The only other thing I knew about him I learned by accident one day when he was out sorting laundry bags with the other two porters. A guard by the name of Strickland peered into our cell with his bulging little eyes to tell me we'd have room inspections in half an hour. He noticed Pepper Pie's Bible tucked under the edge of his mattress, and he did what I was afraid he was going to do—he opened the door. I had been at peace, rolling Bugler into perfect cigarettes and drinking a jailhouse mocha, a teaspoon of instant coffee and a teaspoon of hot chocolate mix. Now I was going to have to look at his mustache, hear his squeaky voice, and smell his rotten cheese breath. "You guys know you can't have anything under your mattresses. Move the book," he said.

"It's my bunkie's Bible. I don't think I should move it."

"I'm not asking you to move it, I'm giving you a direct order."

"You're going to write me a ticket if I don't move someone else's property? Is that a major or a minor ticket?"

"Move the Bible or give me your ID, jackass."

I wanted him out—him and his whole ratlike vibe—so I pulled the book from under the mattress and Strickland closed the door. I held the book in my hand and looked at the cover, a tree in warm orange autumn colors with the sun causing the leaves to glow from behind. The cover was genuine, but the inner pages were too thick: they weren't the usual onionskin pages we rolled our cigarettes with. I opened the book to the middle and found it full of typing paper, folded and cut to fit and glued between the Bible's covers. On every page were two sentences, handwritten in small letters of blue ink:

For as he thinks in his heart, so is he. It shall be done for you as you have believed. The pages were numbered and ended at 452. When I reached the back cover I felt terrible for having the book in my hands, especially knowing what I knew of Pepper in the nighttime. I was quick to cover my tracks—I cleaned off my fingerprints with toilet paper and put the book back under his mattress exactly as I had found it.

If only I'd been as careful with the ketamine.

It's a simple fact that I never sold so much as a taste of the drug. I thought about it, sure—I could have cooked it into powder and sold it as ecstasy for one hundred times what I paid. But try telling the Drug Enforcement Administration that the massive amount of pharmaceuticals you've imported is for personal use. They could care less about how big or small your appetite. After a certain amount, it's distribution by default.

Four months after leasing a new mailbox—this time in Kalamazoo—I saw a long, white Chevy van with tinted side windows pull out of the Taco Bell next door, but they didn't get me then. Later, when they offered to drop federal charges in exchange for a guilty plea, I learned that the second mailbox I had set up as Mr. Gauss triggered a law enforcement alert—two mailboxes in different states under the same name. Meanwhile, I was spending most of my time alone, sliding through slick mechanized cities to arrive at that glowing, glorious destiny.

It was spring 2006, and the baseball season began. I had a TV, Pepper Pie didn't, and he was grateful I liked baseball too. Every night when there was a game, we watched the Detroit Tigers. The year before, they had lost 10 shy of 100 games. Three years prior, they had set an American League record by losing 119, but this year, they had a new coach and were expected to possibly win half of the season.

Our unit, Eastlake, was one of two low-profile, two-story buildings on our half of the compound. Once the snow melted off the grass we began softball practice on the days we had afternoon recreation. I was badly out of shape, but I could catch an outfield fly, which is not as easy as it looks on TV. I played left field. Pepper Pie was a little rusty from the winter, but he played third base and started off batting near the top of the lineup because he had an on-base percentage of .500. He was quick with the glove—great hand-eye coordination—and could generate a lot of bat speed for a small guy.

Pepper and I took softball seriously, constantly helping each other improve. We'd watch the Tigers play, making mental notes and applying the subtleties on the field—keeping the back elbow up in the batter's box, keeping our baseline stride short and sure. We kept statistics and encouraged each other. We were ready for the competitive season to begin against our rivals across the yard, Dublin Unit.

A week before the season began, our slightly overweight second baseman, Frank, was taking batting practice. We would each hit four balls, then run on the fifth. On the fifth pitched ball, Frank hit a nice shot to the gap in left-center. He'd just rounded second on his way to third when his top-heavy body tumbled to the dirt. Al, our shortstop, caught the ball and tagged him out. "His Bugler light came on." Al laughed. "You need to give up the smokes, fat ass."

If it had been anyone but Al, I don't think Frank would have done what he did. But Al had taken the shortstop position from Frank a few weeks earlier because he was just plain better. Frank stood up, dusted off his belly, then spit between Al's eyes. There wasn't much of a choice for either of them after that—they had to fight, or be permanently labeled cowards. Al started swinging, even though he was outweighed by fifty pounds. After any fight, both parties involved spend a month or so in administrative segregation, and then each is moved to a different prison to avoid reprisals. You never see them again.

This meant the Eastlake team was in serious trouble. We had no infield and no number three and four hitters. Frank and Al were good players. We filled the positions with Tex and Sparky, neither of whom could bat his way out of a paper bag and who seemed allergic even to soft grounders. We lost our first seven games.

The Tigers, meanwhile, were establishing the best record in all of baseball. Pepper Pie and I watched nightly, sharing microwave popcorn as night after night a hero emerged—Granderson, Marcus Thames, Brandon Inge, and numerous veterans well past their prime.

Pepper Pie was growing stronger all the while. I'd watch him on the nights he exercised, and eventually got to know his schedule: every third night, unless the end of the month was coming up, when he might rest a few more days so he could begin on the first. His schedule was determined more by the first of every month than by anything else I could figure.

I was going to have to broach the subject soon—he was progressing rapidly, able to stay completely gone for three minutes. As the All-Star break approached, he could push his torso clean through the thick steel of the door, which looked to be more difficult than the glass—he had to push harder, and oftentimes the opposing force made him stumble backward.

Eastlake was becoming very effective at losing, though at least our margins had shrunk since the start of the season. Pepper Pie and I developed the quiet camaraderie that team losership brings, a complement to the camaraderie we'd built by watching the winning Tigers.

They were playing the Yankees in New York one Sunday afternoon after dropping the first of the doubleheader. Late in the game, Craig Monroe hit a home run to win the game. His mother, Marilyn, was in the stands. In a ghostly way, the former wife of Joe DiMaggio was in Yankee Stadium again too.

"Pretty unbelievable, huh?" I said.

"Yeah," Pepper said. "I never thought I'd back a winning team."

We couldn't see each other. I was on the top bunk, and he was on the lower. We were as quiet as the Yankee fans for a moment. Then I asked him.

"You leaving soon?"

"October, probably," he said. "I know you know."

"How?"

"The cover to my Bible was too clean."

"Strickland told me to move it. I panicked and moved it back. I wanted to learn. I'm not going to tell anyone."

"It doesn't matter," he said. I could hear his springs shifting on the bunk below. "No one would believe you, and even if they did, there's nothing they could do. They could keep a guard on me twenty-four-seven, but one night I'll be gone, regardless."

"Is it anything I can learn?"

Talking to someone on your bunk is almost like talking to yourself. I spoke to the ceiling, my hands behind my head. The pause waiting for the other person to reply is a real test of patience: there is no way to gauge how close he is to answering. He might have drifted off to sleep, or in Pepper Pie's case, he could have disappeared.

"Are you still there?"

"I'm thinking," he said.

"Are you able to do it because of the dead man's number they gave you?"

"The number was just the beginning. It allowed me to believe I was different." He stood up to look at me.

"But listen," he said. "You don't want to be able to do this. You got it pretty good here and you'll get out eventually. You got a good number, so you might as well not think about it. Because once you get to where you can walk out of here, once you can walk right through that door, I'm pretty sure you can't come back. From what I can tell, I'm pretty sure you stay disappeared."

"Are you willing to do that?"

"I got no one on the outside, man. There's you in here, but they can move you any minute. Disappearing isn't such a bad thing anyway," he said. "Sometimes I feel like I already have."

Jonnie Rae was never more than a figure on the sidewalk at night. Standing on Park Street, the stained glass of the law office in the background, she was never all the way solid. And now that the memories of her are fading . . . The memory that remains most solid is the last time I saw her, when I ended up at the river, lying in someone else's handmade wooden boat, listening to the water under the hull. Jonnie Rae had said, "Follow me to the river. I think you'll like the music there." The water was humming, of course. It sounded old and deep. There was the surface splashing and rattling against the boat, but you had to listen past that to the river's soul.

Our softball tournament began one week before the World Series. Prison tournaments are magical in a way: all previous losses are erased—theoretically, anyway. The recreation worker raked the field, cut the tall outfield grass, filled in the dips on the infield, and drew chalk foul lines, batter's boxes, and on-deck areas in perfect white circles. New gravel was spread under both benches. Everything was crisp white and brown and green. We all wore our dark blue clothes with orange stripes. Our prison-issued black dress shoes gave better traction on the field, so everyone wore them too. The softballs were brand-new Gold Dots, white and solid. I sat on the bench and watched everyone warming up. Pepper Pie and I had been watching the Tigers all year on a twelve-inch black-and-white screen, and I had forgotten about the beautiful colors of baseball.

We didn't expect to win the tournament; we'd only won two games all season. The Dublin Unit had been talking for weeks about how they were going to spend the five dollars given to each player on the winning team, and we had resigned ourselves to second place.

The tournament was best two out of three, and after losing the first, we won the second game when I hit a deep fly to center field. Tex, who had only recently learned to run the bases *after* the ball was caught, tagged up and scored the winning run. We were to play the final game October 21, opening day of the World Series. But the rain came.

I had the sense that Pepper Pie could go at any time,

but he wanted to finish the softball season and watch the World Series with me. Secretly, I started training myself using the pages of my King James Bible. The cover was a light brown marble design with a cross in raised relief. I spent hours cutting pages away and rolling them into cigarette papers. Every day, I wrote the same verses Pepper Pie had written. He said it would take a year to really believe that all I had to do was believe.

The Tigers lost their first game 7–2, unable to hit a good rookie pitcher in Reyes. It snowed and rained the next day, a Sunday. Rain and snow were forecasted for game time in Detroit that night, but the Tigers played and won, despite a lackluster offensive performance, as well as a possible illegal substance on the throwing hand of the Tigers' pitcher. Sundays are always slow and depressing in prison, but the win brought some light to the day's dreariness.

We were scheduled to play that Monday at 5:50. As the time of the final game approached, I wrote my verses. Pepper Pie lay on his bunk with his eyes closed. He had a tendency to become very nervous before games, so he would visualize performing well. I kept my TV on the Weather Channel to keep track of the time and possible rain. There didn't seem to be any, except down by the Indiana state line. Five-fifty came and went. "Why aren't they letting us out?" Pepper Pie asked.

"I have no idea," I said.

Soon it was 6:00, and Strickland passed by our window on his top-of-the-hour rounds. Pepper Pie jumped out of his bunk and ran to the door. He yelled through the crack: "Hey, Strickland, are we having our game?"

I knew the news was bad when the beady eyes appeared in the glass. If the game was on, he would have simply said so, but because he returned, we knew Strickland had some personal pleasure to indulge in. He looked at us, smiled, and opened the door. "Don't you geniuses know? It's raining."

I had been weaving my pen through the fingers of my left hand. I tapped the TV screen with it. "It shows right here, no rain, genius."

"If you'd look out the window, you'd see," Strickland said. Our windows were at ground level. They were clouded and dirty, so we couldn't see much except a tall light pole, Cyclone fence, and razor wire.

"The point is you could have announced it so we wouldn't be waiting," Pepper said. "You know, if you didn't think of us like rats, you wouldn't look and smell so much like a fucking rat. How about that, genius?"

"All right, 121, you just got yourself an insolence ticket." Strickland shifted his pointy gaze to me. "You too, 573. Now neither of you have to worry about your little softball game because you'll be on sanctions. Season's over, motherfuckers."

Strickland pulled his thick policy directive from his back pocket. The tickets were yellow, and the book looked like a miniature notebook in his hand.

What I should have thought about at that moment were my last few minutes as a free man in that beautiful wooden rowboat. Jonnie Rae sat on one of the boat's benches and we drifted. I had my ear to the hull listening to the very real eternal hum of the river. Then flashlights darted around and I heard someone enter the water, breaking the hum. A beam of light flooded the inside of the boat as we were pulled ashore. I looked around for Jonnie Rae. "Looking for someone?" the cop asked. I thought it was the end. "Goodbye," I said.

But I didn't think about that at all. Strickland wrote out the ticket for Pepper Pie, and I watched my bunkie begin to fade. He tossed the ticket into the toilet and tried to press the flush button, but couldn't. His thumb, then his hand, sunk through the stainless steel. He opened his mouth to talk, but nothing came out. Then he smiled.

"Five seventy-three—give me your ID card," Strickland said. Pepper Pie was nearly gone for good.

"I have a name," I said, standing up and pulling the packet of Bugler from my shirt pocket. I kept already-rolled cigarettes in the tobacco pouch, and my bright yellow ID outside in the fold, along with a book of matches. I stood up to walk to the door. "See, Strickland? Right there on my card, I have a name. And I'm not going anywhere for a while, so why don't you start to use it."

Near the door, I pretended to fumble with the packet, dropping the rolled smokes and matches past the open threshold and into the hall, which I couldn't pass through without permission. Strickland watched me carefully and rather than grant me the liberty to come out and gather them myself he kneeled and collected them for me. I felt a brush of air move past me and through the open door. The season was over, but for some of us, a new one was beginning. "Hello," I said. Hello.

IN THE DAYROOM WITH STINKY

Stinky walks into the room where the men play cards. They play dominoes and talk. They play chess and sell handmade Christmas cards. They smoke in the corner by the window.

It smells like straight-up donkey ass in here, he says. Stinky thinks everything stinks. He says he's got extra-sensitive smelling and he doesn't smell nothin' good.

Stinky in the dayroom: Is that thunder in fucking October? The trees are changing. I think that one's dead though. These planes fly low because they're keeping an eye on me. When I leave, you watch—you won't see no more planes around here.

Stinky sits down across from me, lays a deck of cards on the table. He got some new T-shirts and what he really likes about them is that the tags have been removed, so it's impossible to put them on backward. He was married—still is, technically—to a prostitute he calls Scared Sarah, who took her medication one night with a Wild Turkey chaser, and then the story gets fuzzy. The only indisputable fact is that she disappeared. Scared Sarah had a bad heart. Her teeth fell out because all the enamel was gone.

Nash is out of cigarettes, and his coffee's gone. He's at the next table and may have the flu.

I would like to be able to see movies again.

I hate the loudness here.

I sleep a lot.

I wonder if the four guys playing their vampire role-playing game know that it isn't real. I don't think it's something they consider.

I've gotten used to instant coffee. It's all right.

Most of my friends have killed someone. Most of my friends were notorious once. A couple of them you can see on A&E's *Cold Case Files.* Stinky's case shows half a dozen times a year. A guy behind me thinks my writing looks like Arabic. He locks in 92. I know because I take in laundry, then hand it out. I know where everyone locks. Almost. There are 240 men in this unit.

Is your name Sam? says Stinky. No? Good. I'll hang around killers but not pedophiles.

People here talk way too much. No one cares what they have to say and I really think some people stay here or keep coming back because they like to talk and people on the outside are tired of listening to them. I heard Leonard Cohen once say he spent five years in a monastery and he compared the experience to being a rough stone in a small cloth bag with other rough stones.

The friction between the stones buffs them all to a flat shine. These guys, though, they don't think of prison that way. They think they're here by accident.

The hardest thing to get used to is the play fighting, learning the difference between real violence and two guys acting like kids. For the first couple of years, you turn around at every loud noise.

What's the name of that card game you're playing? Casino, says Stinky. I mean solitary. You mean solitaire? And then he shuffles the deck, lays the cards in thirteen piles of four. He asks me what I think the odds are there are four of a kind in one pile. About a million to one, I say. Then he turns over four aces in the first pile and all the rest in sequential order.

I should have been a card shark, he says. Hey, maybe if we showed that trick to the judge, he'd let us go.

Yeah, maybe.

I think the correct term is card*sharp,* but I've always thought *card shark* was the better description. I would rather be a shark than sharp, though I keep that to myself.

All the old grifters had names for the tricks they used: the Lefty Lucy, the Turn and Run, the Disappearing Deck, the Bloody Valentine, the Bootless Jack. And though Stinky knows a lot of card tricks, he has no names for any of them.

Here are the facts of his case as reported to me by Stinky himself and Bill Kurtis of *Cold Case Files*:

Scared Sarah Brown née Novak and Stinky are married in 1978. She wears white and he pays fifty dollars for a nice, tall wedding cake, which she picks up and throws at him during the reception in the basement of the American Legion Post 714. The wedding gala is attended by a who's who of Kalamazoo County's dealers, pimps, and thieves. The marriage is rocky, and in a couple of years, it's completely on the rocks. There is a well-documented history of domestic incidents with the two of them alternating roles as the aggressor. She passes out nightly with a couple of Valium (she disliked the newer generation of benzodiazepines) and a half pint of Wild Turkey. He takes out a term life policy on her for $100,000, and a month later, she disappears. There is no body—no trace of a body found. Ever. Even to this day. The case goes cold with no insurance being paid because there's no proof Scared Sarah is dead and not in Cancún living on the beach. Six years later, some nutcase barfly named Monica "Deadeye" Silver says on the stand that Stinky told her all about how he smothered Scared Sarah, ran her through a meat grinder he used for venison, then fed her ground remains to a pen of thirty hogs north of town. Stinky says he has never even seen Monica. Her statement comes two weeks before the coroner was to pronounce Scared Sarah presumed dead, the insurance money paid to Stinky.

A brief legal primer: *corpus delecti* literally means "body of a crime." Generally, in a homicide case, there must be proof that someone died and that the deceased came to their end via foul play. Generally, it takes more than a recovered memory from a crazy woman to convict someone. But Michigan is funny that way.

Generally, it takes proof—unless $100,000 is involved, Stinky says. He thinks Scared Sarah most likely died en route south with a guy she probably barely knew. One day Stinky thinks she's in a ditch somewhere between Michigan and Mexico. Another day he thinks she's going to show up alive. Maybe here.

Also, I miss good music. I miss alternative music you can't hear on VH1.

Someone on B-Wing took thirty of something. Thirty what? It don't matter, he took thirty of them. You take thirty of anything and that's a wrap. It's that time of the year. People get depressed. They think enough's enough.

When I get back to court, Stinky says, for my opening statement I'm gonna show the judge a razzle-dazzle card trick that's going to blow his mind.

You've got to come up with a catchy name for it, Stinky. You can't just say to him, Okay, Judge, here's my card trick.

He looks out the window. Snow is possible today, or tomorrow.

A name, huh?

Someone stands up: I'll tell you one thing; I'll tell you this—all that medication they got me waking up for at five-thirty? They can stick it straight up their ass!

The one part of Stinky's story I always get hung up on is this: why get rid of her body if you're trying to collect insurance money? And this too: he still seems stunned that she threw a beautiful fifty-dollar cake at him. It was over thirty years ago.

Judge Peckerneck, for my opening statement, Stinky says he'll say, I'd like to call your attention to this deck of cards for a little something I call Aces-in-the-Middle-Razzle-this-whole-thing-stinks-like-a-monkey-took-a-shit-in-an-old-boat-Dazzle.

Another thing I miss: when I would mow my yard, my dog followed close behind me, and when I would stop, he'd run into the back of my legs. There was something very comforting about that.

It's laundry day. I'm going to take a shower. On the way to lunch Stinky told me good things were going to happen to me today because he prayed for me and my kids for a long time last night. I'm going to take a shower then wait. I'm going to drink strong coffee and wait for good things to happen.

SWANS

A-Ward at the Michigan Reformatory is a converted gym with a peaked roof and a dozen ceiling fans that whip warm air around the eight-man cubes like hot wind from the wings of desert vultures.

The first third of A-Ward is a dayroom with a wall-mounted TV in front of five rows of chairs. There are a dozen circular card tables, two microwaves, two toasters, and an ironing board with an iron that occasionally works and is permanently connected to the wall by the kind of chain old ladies use to keep their glasses around their necks.

Behind the officers' desk there are generally two COs keeping an eye on things, and behind them is the bathroom, with a row of individual showers, toilets, and stainless-steel urinals. I am responsible for scrubbing these urinals Monday through Thursday right after noon count.

Last Tuesday I did not scrub the urinals. It is December and for Christmas, as a present for myself that morning, I traded three bags of instant coffee at $3.15 a piece for a small amount of weed. After doing seven years of a natural life sentence, I bought prison drugs for the first time, unless you count the Faygo bottle full of potato hooch last year, which I could not drink because it smelled and tasted like potato soup left on the stove for a week.

I bought the weed from Russell, a bald, skinny white man missing nearly every tooth between his canines. When he handed me the little folded piece of paper holding the tiny square of familiar dark green, I had to ask him how to light it. I already knew how to roll it, as smoking was allowed until three months ago, and now without rolling papers we used the onionskin wrappers that held our rolls of toilet paper. Sitting beside me on my bunk, he gave me a quick lesson with an AA Energizer and a copper wire stripped from an earphone cord, so thin I had to look twice at his palm to find it.

So last Tuesday, instead of scrubbing the urinals with the frothy, fragrant soap and the worn-out scrubber, I sat on the thin rim of a toilet behind the closed stall door, beneath the exhaust fan ten feet above, and I held the nearly invisible wire to the positive and the metal ground (the battery's body reached by scratching through the label), searing the end of my index finger and thumb. The crimp in the middle of the wire turned red and I lit the toothpick-size joint. I coughed and was briefly dizzy. I flushed the jet-engine-loud toilet, I suppose in order to cover the sound of the cough, albeit too late. The only other person in the bathroom was the shower cleaner, Wilhelm, a short, quiet German man who had pushed his wife from a building in Saginaw. I didn't know him and I didn't want to. He might be a snitch, or worse, he might knock on the door and want a hit.

In a moment, the joint was done, the roach flushed, the battery and wire in my pocket. I washed my hands then went to the front row of seats to watch the last fifteen minutes of the twelve o'clock news. At 12:30, count would be cleared, then chow called.

Watching the news was my daily routine, only now I was high. The minutes passed, and a tingly blanket slowly wrapped around my body while my mind alternated colors, switching from dark paranoia to bright, absurd hilarity. I tried to focus on the news but a feeling of unhinged laughter had broken out somewhere above my knees, a place I had forgotten about.

The weatherman seemed to be talking directly to me: "It'll be cold, but very sunny today—you'll want your knit hat, as well as your sunglasses." He seemed like an old buddy genuinely concerned about my being prepared for the day. When the weather was over, the scene shifted to a lake, placid and bright, surrounded by beautiful homes. According to the anchor, the Michigan Department of Natural Resources had spent the morning out there culling swans with twelve-gauge shotguns. The camera shot tight on a white Ford pickup with a windowed bed cover. The shot moved tighter still, through the back window and into a pile of at least fifty stone-cold swans, which looked to me like a pile of surreal pillows on the way to a fairy-tale home for orphans.

An emotional monologue began from a local lady—pretty, middle-aged, exactly the sort of woman you would expect to see gardening outside one of those beautiful homes on the lake. She had tears in her eyes. "I know they have to control the swan population," she said, "because of disease or whatever. I just question the methods." The scene flashed to a couple of pump-action shotguns leaning against the front bumper of the white DNR pickup. "They just came out without telling anyone and then . . . bam, bam, bam." She made the universal sign for a handgun with her index finger and thumb and jerked it back through several recoils.

I loved the way she couldn't speak of death. I loved how she could only act it out, miming the entirely wrong symbol for the guns they actually used. It was perfect for her—girlish, innocent, somehow sexy. She had never made that sign before. She'd never had to.

Behind her, the camera zoomed in on a thin stream of syrupy blood snaking through the gate of the truck and puddling on the corner of someone's white concrete driveway.

But the final shot of the story, in calming opposition to the violence, was a scene of a dry creek bed spanned by a long bridge, some faded, illegible graffiti tag written on the side of its I-beam. The camera panned slowly through the black branches of the bare winter trees to a shot of the cold, glimmering lake, radiant, not a swan in sight.

I hadn't gone with the camera, though. I had stayed with the graffiti, under that bridge, which in my current state I was certain was a bridge I'd known back in high school, the graffiti freshly painted by my buddy, Ricky. It was a Zeppelin lyric—*Have you seen the bridge?*—scrawled in bright orange spray paint, still wet and dripping as Ricky walked from the bank, smiling and rubbing his fingers on his jeans, smearing paint in a permanent dull smudge.

Crash was with us, as he always was when we ditched school for his shack during lunch break. He'd brought us down to the river to show us his latest project. "They mate for life, you know," he said, talking about the swan, *his* swan. Not dead, but brand-new and very much alive as it swam in confused, abbreviated circles in the center of the dirt-brown Little Wabash River. Apparently, he was going to breed them.

A couple of things should be said about Crash. First, there was some dispute that his nickname was actually Chunk, but had evolved over time into something less offensive. In 1979, after a Flatlanders Motorcycle Club party, he had missed a curve on his Harley and was found the next morning broken in half, heels wrapped around the back of his head, rendering his legs useless along with everything else below his severed spine. He had become a "chunk" of flesh. He drove around in a specially equipped van, and spent his first disability checks not on something practical like wooden ramps up to the shack just a few feet away from where we sat under the bridge but on a thousand dollars' worth of Swiss-made speakers no one could pronounce the name of. He also would not reveal where or how he'd gotten them, as if they were a secret of national importance.

It was said he used to be strong. Those who knew him before told stories of how he used to show off under the bridge, how he could hang by his fingertips and traverse any of the four massive, fifty-foot-long I-beams. Some said he could *still* traverse the span, and in fact his upper body still appeared strong, but should he drop into the Little Wabash thirty feet below, the current would carry him away so quickly he would drown. He had lost his sense of adventure after the accident anyway—what with the surgeries, and the unfaithfulness of Sheila, his wife.

"Not only do they mate for life," he said, "but they're fucking *loyal*."

Another thing to be said about Crash: during any discussion, no matter the subject, at some point he would come around to the fact that wives, and all women, were unfaithful. It was universally known among us high school degenerates that this was to be agreed with, and Crash to be given free conversational rein in general, because somewhere, hidden around the sandy yet fertile clay soil of the once–river bottoms, Crash grew the most potent marijuana this side of South America.

The way Crash told it, five years prior, in 1981, he was traveling to Bike Week with the Flatlanders and had come across some seeds in Daytona, direct descendants of a potent strain from the mountains of Afghanistan. The weed smelled like skunk spray, could cause the uninitiated smoker to cry or vomit or both, and it cost fifty dollars for a quarter ounce—double what the usual Colombian went for. But Crash's Afghani was worth it. Even hippies who had been smoking pot for longer than Ricky and I had been alive could get high on one hit.

We drove back to school in Ricky's car, a '78 Trans Am with a shot suspension that rattled loudly over any bump, especially the bricks of the town square. The T-tops were out and a mess of burnout paraphernalia swung from the rearview mirror: a red headband, a purple Crown Royal bag holding hemostats stolen from the hospital, and a black lacy garter. Ricky had a habit of using much too much Armor All on the interior vinyl, so if you weren't paying attention you could slide right out of the seat if he stopped too quickly.

"How about that swan?" I asked him.

"That's the last swan you'll see," he said. "I mean, that's the last one he'll get. Remember his plan to grow all of his own food?"

"That ended up as a pumpkin patch and row of okra?"

"And the plan to build a house on stilts after we got that big rain."

"And then how he was going to become famous for discovering a new planet with that big-ass telescope that he watches Cindy Cleary with?"

We got back to school just as the bell rang for fifth period. There were plenty more of his plans we could have listed: the moonshine still on a working submarine, generating his own electricity from a waterwheel built on the river. Without a doubt this was all due to the sheer power of his marijuana, plus all the free time on his hands. Now he was breeding swans because they exhibited the faithfulness and beauty he had tried and failed to find in people.

Where had he even gotten the swan? I wondered before sixth-period American History. And, was a swan even supposed to be in a river? I had only seen them on ponds and lakes. Wouldn't the swan fall asleep and drift down with the current, never to be heard from again?

It didn't matter. By the end of the day we had forgotten about the swan.

The next week we hopped in the Trans Am, the black interior steaming from a day in the sun, and rolled down Route 45, past the tall grain silos of the Louisville Seed House, the park, down the south edge of the brick square just below the courthouse, and on to Crash's narrow drive, past his conversion van and down the steep road of the riverbank to sit in the car in the shade of the bridge. There were half a dozen swans scuttling around the sand on the bank of the swollen springtime river.

Before Ricky killed the engine Crash was out his back door, zigzagging down the wooden stairs on his metal crutches. He could descend those stairs as fast as an able-bodied man, though to watch him do it was nerve-racking. It was like a controlled fall, the way his feet trailed behind him like the tail of a kite. Crash crutched over to our passenger-side door and pulled a joint from the pocket of his sleeveless flannel shirt. "Fire it up," he said. "What do you think of them?"

"It sounds like your secret Swiss speakers going berserk," said Ricky. Half a dozen swans were honking and hissing aggressively to one another about the Trans Am in their midst. They seemed to be hatching a scheme to kill us.

"They'll fight to the death for the ones they love," he told us, and the next week there were six more, transported in his van from the egg farm seven miles south of town. The farm had twenty of them, he said, and was practically giving them away after their experiment with swan eggs hadn't panned out. But apparently there were laws governing the sale of livestock—a person couldn't just buy twenty of anything, but had to purchase them in groups determined by some Department of Conservation formula. They were ten dollars apiece, and by the end of April we were looking at, and listening to, and fearing, two hundred dollars' worth of swans. Two hundred dollars' worth of noisy, dirty, aggressive birds that as far as Ricky and I were concerned had really fucked up our quiet pot-smoking hideout.

The key to the beginning of the end of the swans, I believe, was tattooed on Crash's left bicep: "Sheila" with the red outline of a heart surrounding the name. No one knows why, but it is a universal law as certain as gravity that the minute you apply permanence to anything in this world, the end begins. It was true with Sheila (and everyone else whose name was tattooed on someone else's body), and just as true when Crash commissioned a mystical swan airbrush painting on the side of his conversion van. Painted onto the side door was a flock of galactic, time-and-space-traveling swans, some of which were coupling but most of them trailing flame from their tail feathers as they rocketed through the dark universe to distant, heart-shaped planets. The writing was on the proverbial wall.

Of course, Ricky and I had discussed killing the swans ourselves; it was a regular topic of conversation as we cruised the country roads around Louisville. Swans would be easy targets—they don't run from you, just the opposite, they engage intruders immediately. They may be beautiful, graceful creatures at a distance, but inside their territory they're brash, violent, and very wild. They guard their ground fiercer than most dogs bred for that purpose. In weed-fueled ramblings inside Ricky's Trans Am we deduced that their territorial nature is likely the reason that they mate for life: their mate, they feel, is their territory.

Still, anyone willing could kill the lot of them with a baseball bat in a matter of minutes.

As much as we hated the swans, we wouldn't hurt Crash by killing them. He loved those birds, and showed anyone who came around the intricate symbolism of the swans on his van, the points of pure white in the vast, dark emptiness of space. There was a bridge in the picture, from the moon to infinity, or at least to the edge of the passenger-side door. It had something to do with bridging the gap between imagined, timeless love and the reality of that ideal exemplified by the swans. That's what Crash said, anyway, when he philosophized about the van after two joints of his Afghani.

The paint still smelled when the first swan died. It didn't yet seem mysterious—a rogue swan had found its way up to the road and was struck by a car, knocked back over the edge of the bridge to the sand below. That Saturday night we had come to get Crash to buy us alcohol; we found him pulling himself and his lifeless legs in haphazard figure eights, his metal crutches strapped to his arms. His head was hanging as if he searched the ground for something he'd lost. He was grieving—killing time waiting for us, or anyone, to dig the hole, which we did. Then we got high and prepared for the eulogy by blasting "Stairway to Heaven" from his Swiss speakers pointed out his back windows. The whole scene was awkward and we were impatient for it to end. We knew we wouldn't be getting any alcohol.

"I don't know what to say," Crash said under the bridge, standing over the bird in his fresh grave about two feet deep. There was not much sign of injury, except that one of his webbed feet was snapped, barely remaining attached. "His name was Bachmann, and he liked sleeping up in the corner of the bridge."

"Well, yeah," I said. "I like that part of the bridge too. That shelf up there—it was cool until they started shitting all over it."

I could feel Ricky glaring at me, but Crash stayed

focused on the grave. He coughed—to clear his mind, I guess—then he was quiet, which made me nervous. Silence always seemed so hazardous when high, and especially with Crash you never knew—he could erupt in fury or break down in tears. But he did neither. "These swans have given me more than I could ever give them," he said. "Amen."

"Amen," Ricky and I said in unison.

Outside of their surly dispositions and the greasy green turds they left everywhere, we hated the swans for another reason. Our high school graduation was coming up, and the places to throw a party around such a small town were limited. Because we knew Crash, and because we were probably his best customers, we had begun working on him a year prior to use his property for a legendary Class of '86 blowout. He had agreed, finally, in January—a huge coup on our part. Crash's place was strategically located to avoid cops. Partyers could park on the square or at the skating rink and walk down—from the street there would be no signs of a party whatsoever. We had a band coming but the acoustics of the concrete bank would shoot the sound eastward, out of town.

But then the swans had come and they were horrible hosts. If the prissy girls from our class came, they wouldn't stay long with huge birds nipping their asses. But we wanted to throw that party more than we would ever admit to each other. On some level, we knew that the forty-seven classmates we had spent the majority of our lives with, we would never see again after that night. If asked, we would have said we didn't care if anyone came, we never liked most of them anyway, but we did care, a lot. Somehow I think we knew when we got older we would think about them, wonder where they were, and what they had done with their lives. At least a small part of our teenage brains knew this last night was important.

After our swan funeral, we didn't see Crash until the next Friday, exactly one week before graduation. We'd pretty much given up hope on the party, ceding that territory to the swans. Crash sat in his wheelchair beside the open passenger door of his van. He seemed paler than usual, and more stoned than usual, staring across the road at nothing. The swans on his van seemed darker still, outside the ring of his porch light, flying toward planets that now looked dark and depressing.

"Something's happening," he said. "Something's wrong."

To be honest, at age eighteen my thoughts were not immediately of concern for Crash's troubles, but about the possible rekindling of the party. He pulled a flask from a side pocket of his wheelchair and took a swig. I realized I had never seen Crash drink. I had seen him trip on mushrooms and acid, had seen him snort small dunes of various powders, even seen him shoot liquid the color of river water into his vein, but I'd never seen him drink.

"The swans," he said. "They caught something. First they're crazy, and then they're dead. One by one, they go crazy and die. The sound they make, it's awful, man . . ."

Now that I listened for it, I could hear. The sound was nearly human, tortured and slow, not the usual bursts of honking that we had come to hate. "Come on," he said, and we all began the awkward trek down to the river.

Half of the swans were scattered around, already dead, the other half lay on the ground shuddering like they were hooked to an electrical outlet. A few twirled in circles in the sand, as if trying to dig their own graves. It was only a matter of time for them.

"It might be contagious," I said.

"Of course it's contagious," Crash said.

"I mean to people, to us."

His back porch light was on, but it was still fairly dark down there. The mosquitoes were thick and relentless for our blood. I was worried about the one swan we had buried a week ago. We hadn't used any gloves. He had died, we thought, at the grille of a car, but in light of all the disease around us, it seemed like we could be taking our last sane breaths. "Why didn't you call someone?" Ricky asked. "A vet or something?"

"I don't have a phone."

"You've got a fucking van, don't you?" Ricky said, sounding just like his lawyer dad. Ricky may have fallen far from one of the few prominent trees in town, but every once in a while—as much as he wanted to deny it—the budding executive came out, along with a leader's short fuse for idiocy. "You've got diseased fucking swans in our river, Crash. Where do you think our water comes from?" He stomped off, up the bank.

"Everything goes downriver," he shouted as he reached the top.

Crash and I looked at each other. He might be in trouble, much more trouble than any of his illegal substances could bring—here and now, people might die of diseased water. I could hear Ricky coming back down the stairs. I wasn't going to let him yell at Crash again, no matter how much he deserved it. He wasn't coming down to yell though, he was carrying the gas can Crash used for starting campfires.

We found gloves in the van and wrapped our faces in Harley-Davidson handkerchiefs. We were careful not to touch the birds. We used poles fashioned from tree limbs to knock the twenty-four swans into a pile. We didn't want to kill the living swans, especially not in front of Crash, who insisted on watching us from the bottom of his steps. But we had no choice when they wouldn't stay in the pile. As easy as it had been to talk about, when it came time to step on their bodies and line up a clear head shot for the sticks, it was very different. They kept moving and moaning, finally Crash handed me the hatchet we'd used to make the poles. By then we were looking to get it all over with, so we lopped their heads off without a second thought. We tapped their severed, seemingly hollow noggins into the pile with the poles, like some surreal golf game. We soaked them with the gasoline, let it sink in for five minutes, and then soaked them again. Without any fanfare, Ricky tossed a match onto the edge of the dirty white pile of swans.

They burned bright and fast. There was a lot of popping involved, I remember, like green twigs tossed on a campfire. There were sounds like that of liquid escaping, of internal gases roiling. Watching them, I was afraid some might explode, but they didn't. They just burned.

We all watched the fire as if it were any other bonfire and not a big pile of birds. Crash finished his flask with a long pull and a loud growl from the whiskey burn. He put on his crutches and ambled off toward the bridge, which was nicely lighted—almost theatrical—from the burning swans, that absurd Zeppelin lyric flickering. He left his crutches at the bottom of the concrete embankment, then dragged himself up the concrete by scooting backward on his ass. "Crash!" Ricky said, his voice reverberating in the perfect acoustics of the bridge. "We're leaving. I know what you're thinking of doing."

"He's going to kill himself," I whispered, more to myself than Ricky.

"I think that's the point."

"Leave, then!" Crash said, sizing up the I-beam.

"For fuck's sake," Ricky said, "If he dies I'm dumping his ass on that fire." Ricky ran over to the embankment, which was pointless, I thought. If we wanted to, we could have stopped him as he crawled up like an inchworm. But it was too late now, and I knew it was all for show. If Crash really wanted to kill himself he would, but there was no reason for him to do this in front of us now, except for the fact that he didn't really want to die.

Crash's strong hands scrambled along the narrow

ledges of the beam. He was dangling far above the flat sandy beach in a couple of seconds. He could probably make it across, I thought, hopefully. But as he got over the river, he lost steam. Ricky had given up, and we watched Crash dangling in the glow of his beloved, diseased swans. His legs hung like a marionette with his strings cut.

"Everything I love," Crash said, "turns to shit." His shoulders began to shake, either from fatigue or sobs, then, without another word, he dropped into the river. There was a splash, then nothing.

We ran to the steep riverbank, the water three feet below. With the onset of summer the river had turned sluggish and low, unlike months ago, when it had swollen to several times its current size. In the light from the swans we spotted him when, like a pale, greasy bobber, he broke the murky surface. Ricky jumped in and pushed him toward the bank. I leaned down and pulled him up.

Crash lay on the sand and coughed up two or three mouthfuls of Little Wabash water. He'd lost his baseball cap in the river and without it he looked like a wet cat. His long hair was much sparser than I'd imagined, and his bright white scalp underneath was misshapen and badly scarred from his accident. His shrunken legs were limp and lifeless in the dying light of the swan fire. He eventually caught his breath, and with his arms around our shoulders, we walked him over to his steps, where he sat with his head in his hands.

There is something that happens when you hang with

guys like Crash, guys who live alone, free of parents, school, and any other responsibility. They make you believe that life can be fun and amazing forever, that they've got it all figured out. But when you realize they don't, when that fuck-all front crumbles and you see them at their weakest, you know you can never go back, that whatever weed is left in your bag will be the last, because the magic is gone for everyone and it'll never seem as sweet again.

None of us caught what killed the swans. I had a rash on both forearms that I thought might be the beginning of something, but by Sunday it was gone. We did not have the Class of '86 party at Crash's. As far as we were concerned, the grounds were contaminated, possibly forever. Our own Chernobyl.

We had the graduation party in an empty cow pasture on the family farm of one of our classmates. A bonfire and the Trans Am's sound system was the focal point. There was a large, iced keg of Budweiser, and as we all got drunker, a few of our classmates began prying old, dry cow patties from the ground and tossing them onto the fire, where they would burn brightly, snapping and popping like those burning swans the week before. At about midnight, the crowd started to thin. I brought the pretty, hyperachiever valedictorian, Lisa Tolliver, another beer. She was leaning against the Trans Am. On the tape deck, Joe Walsh was singing about how everybody's so different, while he hasn't changed, life's been good to him so far. We touched plastic cups in a lame toast, then

I tried to coax her into taking a hit off a joint of Crash's Afghani. I was curious—would she cry? Vomit? Both? Would she press her Princeton-bound breasts against me, then kiss me passionately against the back spoiler of Ricky's car?

But Lisa didn't do any of those things. She finished her beer, then handed me her empty cup. She told me she didn't need drugs to escape. She hoped that someday I would get to a place where I didn't need to escape either.

THE WORLD OUT THERE

Rentería almost hits one out in the bottom of the ninth of a 3–3 game against Cleveland. It's been a nightmare season of almosts for Detroit. Still, I watch them every single night. Inge pops up to second and a cameraman zooms in on a young woman: pretty, her hair bleached blond from the summer, dark skin and studs in her ears, legs propped up on the seat in front of her. She's wearing a college sweatshirt, a Big Ten school, though I'm not sure anyone still calls it the Big Ten anymore. Next to her is a boy, her boyfriend, I figure. And next to him is his brother, their mom and dad. It's obvious the four of them are related, just as obvious that she's not. She is texting someone, a girl, her best friend, Marcie, could be. She's texting Marcie about the classes she's taking first semester, which begins in a couple weeks at the Big Ten school represented in large letters across her shirt. She keeps typing as the game goes into extra innings. *Sure, I'm scared,* she writes Marcie. *But I'm excited too.*

An Indian hits a home run in the top of the tenth.

They didn't have texting when I was on the outside. I understand the concept, though. I talk by phone to people out there. I have a fourteen-year-old son, who, according to his mother, "texts his life away." I taught the boy to box when he was younger. Now he trains at a famous gym in Portland and I write him letters. It's all I can do.

They go to the bottom of the tenth. Cleveland's up by one.

Do they have a little typewriter pad like my old electronic dictionary, or is it a regular numbered pad where you flip through the corresponding letters? I understand the concept, but not the specifics.

Yet I know what the almost coed is typing to her BFF. She's going to dump his ass as soon as she gets to college. *I mean, he's nice and all, we've had fun, but I'm like, eighteen.* She doesn't type the obvious: how pretty she is, how doors just seem to open, how she'll have a million friends and guys calling her, texting her, how she'll go to parties and not remember him, how she'll forget all of this. But her grades will be good and she'll either fall in love for real or go to law school. It'd be a different story if Steve or Joey, Sinbad or whatever his name is (she's already starting to forgot), if he were going to the Big Ten school too. But he couldn't even get in.

Actually, he didn't even apply. He thinks he fooled her by getting the application, talking to her in detail about what he was writing on the essay. He says he's going to apply again next year, until then he's going to junior college, but he's not even 100 percent on that. To her it's obvious—he knows he's never going to college, junior or otherwise.

The Tigers go down easily, three up, three down. They lose again. They're not even going to finish this year at .500. He doesn't know yet she's going to dump him. He still thinks she likes baseball. She doesn't. It's boring, stupid. She will never like baseball, ever.

The game ends and people are leaving, going home. She texts goodbye to Marcie, who is not going to the Big Ten school in the fall either, but that's different. She and Marcie will always be best friends. No question.

He takes her hand and she lets him. They leave Comerica Park, and she smiles at him, even, thanking him for taking her tonight. She'll let him believe in something awhile longer, because she'll forget about this night pretty soon. He won't. He'll keep the ticket stub. He'll enjoy watching that kid Cabrera, who's knocked in a hundred runs every year his first three seasons in the majors, who'll get to the Hall of Fame if he stays healthy.

The girl's phone buzzes. She lets go of his hand and types a few words, coded, no doubt, like the language of wartime spies. I can understand the concept, though it's beyond my ability to ever perform. Like texting would be if I were out in the world. All these people, typing on their little keypads with ease. But some of us just can't get it, and after a while we don't even try anymore. We're out of touch, in our own world. We sit there in love while she's already written the end in a sparse, abbreviated language we will never understand.

SIX PICTURES OF A FIRE AT NIGHT

One long and dangerously hot summer my friend Catfish cleaned the homes of suicides in Grand Rapids. Then he finds himself in prison, and the classification lady finds out about his earlier summer job. So when some elderly inmate two weeks from release wedges his head under the wheel of an idling semi behind the chow hall and waits for the truck to take off, they have Catfish clean it up. He's the go-to guy now for the messes people make at our facility. All hours, day or night, like a doctor. Catfish.

I asked him once how many people he cleaned up during that one summer on the outside.

"A lot," he said. "It was hot, like a hundred degrees for three months straight."

"How many is a lot?" I asked. We were at a table by the softball field waiting for the energy to exercise. All we'd done so far was smoke five cigarettes.

"Have you ever seen the mess a shotgun in the mouth makes? Really, man, one is a lot."

This is true of course, but he knew I wanted numbers.

He shrugged. "A dozen, fifteen tops."

Catfish is half Mexican and half Irish. He's short with a long, bald head and widely spaced teeth, the whole effect making him look like a homely extraterrestrial. He was in prison because he took his wife fishing, killed her, and sunk her in the lake. That's his case, at least. I've read his transcripts—all three hundred pages—but I don't remember the name of the lake or the name of the small town it was near.

What I remember most about the transcripts is that his public defender put him on the stand in his own defense. His defense was that they fought, she died, he panicked and weighted her down with some bricks he found along a secluded bank. The worst part of the three-day trial occurred when the prosecutor asked him what he did after he'd sunk her. "I kept fishing for catfish," he said. Even reading the scripts, I could see the jury: twelve middle-aged white people, their mouths collectively open, revealing the small black holes of the accused's future. I doubt they even paid attention after that.

I'll just come right out and say it: I don't think Catfish killed his wife. I'm pretty sure his sister killed her because the wife stole her crack, and Catfish took the rap. On and off for the past year I've tried to get him to admit it. I'm not sure why, except I don't think he should carry that weight all alone. He won't do it, though. He'll talk around the subject, about how his sister and his wife really hated each other, about how they both loved to smoke crack, and once he said, "Mary stole—" and that was it. He stopped himself.

So we got off the table finally, at the same time, like a couple of birds that agree to fly away without a sound between them. It was the first day of March and we needed to get back in shape. It was cold still but there were twenty or so guys walking around the asphalt track.

We walked in silence for a few minutes then stopped and did twenty push-ups on the grass near the guard tower. It was sunny but there were still patches of snow around the yard. We walked awhile longer and after our second set of push-ups he told me there's a serial shower crapper on B-Wing. "About once every three days, they call me to clean it up."

I asked if he'd rather clean up crap in a shower or suicides. "Suicides, definitely," he said. "After three or four, it's no worse than—I don't know—cleaning a bunch of fish. With suicides you wear a respirator and it's mostly a bunch of scraping. It's the same thing all over the room, brain and bone, sometimes parts of teeth. You think of something else. You can be putting the last of a guy's head in a bag thinking of who Detroit's playing tonight, whether Rentería is going to come out of his slump, what you've got to pick up for dinner."

We did our third set of push-ups. My arms were starting to feel a little rubbery, but I wanted to get at least one hundred in, and at least three miles. As we warmed up we took off our coats, state-issue blue with a bright orange stripe down the arms and back.

About half the homes he cleaned were middle-class: nice and neat, except for the room, usually a smaller room, like a closet or basement. The other half of the homes were dirty, messy with signs of obsession such as stacks and stacks of every issue ever of a magazine. The homes of the mentally ill. They smelled different, he said. They were dark. The shades were drawn.

The last home he cleaned was a house trailer. Dirty dishes everywhere, Catfish said, not just in the kitchen but the bathroom and bedroom, the bathtub, oven, the fridge.

There were three piles five feet high of *Scientific American*. There were full ashtrays of Kools. A small TV sat in front of a well-worn recliner. A police scanner occupied a TV tray to the left of the chair alongside an empty bottle of champagne that the man used as a candleholder. There was a half-burned yellow candle smelling of butterscotch when Catfish went to clean.

And then the room. There was always the room. "You're told which one and where it is, but you can smell it first without the respirator on. Especially when it's hot. It's not rotten, so much as a cross between gunpowder and old hamburger meat," he said.

His boss, Cindy, would stand outside the white panel van equipped with five-hundred-gallon tanks of cleaning solution and hot water, huge coils of thick gray hoses, levers and switches on a complicated control panel. It was a van-size vacuum cleaner powered by a mufflerless diesel generator, the sound of which let everyone within a mile know something serious was taking place. The fifty-foot hose snaked from the van to Catfish's long steam nozzle, which sprayed hot, sanitizing cleaner on the forward pass, then vacuumed the now-bloody solution on the pull back. The hose coiled then released like a python as it sprayed and vacuumed, vacuumed and sprayed. His boss ate Cheetos while Catfish worked, staining her fingers the fluorescent orange of a traffic cone.

The man had killed himself in his bedroom. It must have been a side-aimed pistol shot because the mess was on the wall, as opposed to the ceiling, indicating a barrel in the mouth. The cleaning was ordinary, except for the pictures on the wall: six of them in glossy color, eight by ten, framed in glass. They were a series of one event with the time and date each one was taken written in the white ink of a gel pen on the lower left corner. Catfish knew right away what the series recorded.

PICTURE 1: 1/15/01, 8:32 P.M.

Outside the door of the suicide's trailer, a glow in the sky many miles away. Catfish remembered seeing that glow from his own house, how it was preceded by a low rumble and a flicker of the lights. His TV went off and everyone in the neighborhood went outside. He thought a jet had crashed somewhere around Gerald R. Ford International, and he knew then why he'd dreamed for years about all manner of aircraft disintegrating before his eyes—once or twice a year, ever since he was a kid.

In the dreams the sky was full of them, all flying in a frenzy, until suddenly they didn't, and he'd watch them fall one by one in a fiery trail. He was watching people die, he knew. Why planes? he'd often wondered, until this rumble and glow led him out that cold night. He was nervous but also excited as he got in his car and drove south toward the glow.

PICTURE 2: 1/15/01, 8:47 P.M.

This one had considerably more of the man stuck to the glass. Catfish sat on the bed, and with a soft rubber scraper he slid the viscous matter into the red biohazard bag then cleaned the picture with bleach wipes.

The picture was taken without flash through the front window of the man's car. The glow is closer now. There's a line of cars ahead of him. As Catfish drove closer to the site, he knew for sure it was definitely not a building. There were only fields for miles and miles. The perfect place for a jet to crash.

PICTURE 3: 1/15/01, 9:15 P.M.

Fire, fifty to a hundred feet high over the tops of trees. Catfish looked for the detritus of a plane crash: seats, luggage, scattered contents of bright white socks and shirts and underwear. He looked for wreckage. He looked for something he would remember forever: a lady's wig blowing across the field, a hand on the road, a laptop that had turned itself on glowing next to the road. But there was nothing yet. He rolled down the window and heard the loud, shrill scream of what may or may not have been a jet engine still running. He smelled fuel of some kind.

PICTURE 4: 1/15/01, 9:27 P.M.

The fourth picture is bright and beautiful. A long, clean flame shooting straight into the air. The only darkness to contrast the overwhelming fire is the bodies of the onlookers at the bottom of the frame. Catfish could have been one of these people, his hands over his ears, leaning slightly forward, as if trying to soak in some of the heat or light. It wasn't a jet crash after all but some sort of exploded gas transfer area. People in silver suits walked toward the fire.

I asked Catfish if he was disappointed that it wasn't a plane.

"Relieved, mostly. Some dreams, you know, you don't want to run into."

PICTURE 5: 1/15/01, 9:43 P.M.

A hole in the upper-right corner, small caliber, maybe a .22. The glass was shattered and there was no way to decontaminate it. Brain, hair, skin, and blood. The picture had been taken driving away, the glow at about the same intensity as driving toward. If you didn't know about the event, if the photo was not part of a series, it would have been meaningless. Catfish slipped the photo from the frame and into a separate biohazard bag. It still hangs, he thinks, on the wall in the home where he used to live, in the home where his mess of a sister lives now.

PICTURE 6: 1/15/01, 10:32 P.M.

Two hours after the first. The same view as picture number 1, except there's no glow. A quarter moon has risen in its place. A chunk of ear stuck to the glass of this one, though cartilage and bone look a lot alike.

When Catfish came home from seeing the fire his wife was watching it on the news. Her name was Mary and that night she wasn't smoking crack. She was drinking Popov out of the bottle. She offered the bottle to him when he walked in, and he took a big drink, then another. He handed it back. She said he smelled like oil or something, and she told him to turn out the lights to see if he glowed. He didn't glow but she capped the bottle, dropping it to the carpet floor, undressed him and pushed him onto the couch. She tied his hands behind his back with his belt and wouldn't let him move. Cheap vodka always made her aggressive.

We finished the last of our push-ups and I think we probably walked over three miles, but I stopped counting laps after a while.

Sometimes you only get one chance, and right then was mine. He would have told me what I already knew. It might have been as easy as saying his name. Or I could couch it in easily deniable terms such as "Your sister made a mess and you had to clean it up, right?" He would have nodded, I think, happy to have one other person in the world that knew.

But it's not so easy to know when a chance like that is passing.

"It's not too bad out here as long as you keep moving," I said.

"How many laps did we do, you think?"

"A dozen, at least."

"We need to do this every day," he said, lighting up a cigarette, subtly acknowledging that we would not do this every day.

I was thinking about that fire and about how Catfish must have felt he was driving to his destiny, no matter how horrible it was. After all those years dreaming about crashing jets, he was headed toward his dream come true. Then, as if he was thinking about the same thing, he said, "Maybe I was a little disappointed." We walked in the direction of our unit. "Not that I wanted anyone to die, understand."

I understood.

DEPAKOTE MO

His name was Maurice. A new guy in the cell next to mine. We could still smoke when I met him.

This was during the Great Tobacco Fiasco of 2009, after the state issued a mandate to phase out smoking in Michigan prisons. The amount of tobacco we could buy from the commissary was slowly dwindling down to none by the end of the year. In theory, stepping down was the way to stop, but addiction and theory work together about as well as children and fireworks.

Our block had seen an ever-increasing list of casualties and vanishings due to the rationing. Maurice replaced a thin, white man named Doo-Wop, a lifelong smoker who by November found himself deep in debt. By then we could buy just a single two-ounce pouch of Bugler a week. But Doo-Wop hadn't cut back his smoking at all, buying pouches inflated at ten times the normal $2.50. The nonsmokers had banded together to form a brutal black market. Debt-laden addicts were regularly beaten up by clean-lunged thugs.

The nonsmokers let Doo-Wop run up his bill because they knew he was good for it. He'd been in the same cell, at the same kitchen job for a decade. You could ask anybody and they'd tell you, Doo-Wop is an old-school convict—a stand-up guy, his word gold. But two nights ago he locked up, which means he walked up to a CO and said, I owe a bunch of money and I'm afraid. After that they have to protect you. They put you in the hole until a bed is found at another prison. Slim said, "At least he's stopped smoking now." It was true, but inside I shuddered to think about quitting cold turkey down in segregation.

As for me, I owed $150, but I was paying it down steady with my hustle: tattoos and hand-painted cards. This was the boom time of year too—Christmas cards. My most popular card this year sold for $2. It was Snoopy wearing a glittery Santa suit with an armful of gifts and Woodstock perched on his shoulder. I'd been drawing Peanuts characters since grade school.

I'd invested twenty dollars in supplies from a mail-order catalog: card stock, glitter, paint, and glue. I figured I could triple that easily over the season, then buy some more Badger calligraphy ink for tattoos and be out of debt by spring. Badger was the only ink we could get, and it was decent but expensive. I'd tried other options on myself—ink from a Bic, a needle through typewriter ribbon, and acrylic paint that my skin rejected in painful, itchy welts. I had been out of Badger for a month, and the best thing I'd come up with since was burning bergamot hair grease inside my locker, letting the threads of black smoke rise and collect into a thick, oily soot that I mixed with spit until it was the consistency of used motor oil.

I had made enough of this for Homer's tattoo when Slim—my bunkie and lookout—said someone was coming down the hall with his duffel bag. "And his head's wrapped in something," he said.

"Like a turban?" Homer asked. He'd just told me he wanted a "13½" on his left arm. 13½ is code for an inmate who had twelve fuckhead jurors, one shithead judge, and a half-assed defense attorney, adding up to a life sentence. I know for a fact Homer never had a trial—he'd taken a plea deal for operating a meth lab. But I'm not in a position to do background checks for tattoos. I owed Homer twenty-five dollars for one pouch of Bugler and the "13½" was going to wipe my slate clean. With him, anyway.

Slim didn't answer. He just told us to be quiet and I shut off the cassette motor that powered my needle. The man who passed looked like just another inmate to me. I noticed his head, though. It was wrapped in white gauze with a few inches of afro sticking out of the gaps. "Hey," Slim said. "What happened to your head?"

"Burned." His cell door opened electronically.

"How do you burn your own head?"

I had seen a lot of men come to prison wrapped in gauze, but it was usually the hands wrapped up in thick white mittens, a mistake in a meth lab.

The new neighbor walked into his cell and didn't say

anything. "Chatty guy, ain't he?" said Slim, before he walked next door. Our cells were open from 7:00 a.m. until 10:00 at night, a sort of pseudofreedom to make up for our lack of access to the yard outside.

The thing about homemade tattoo ink was that it kept clogging the Bic barrel. I had the standard setup: a motor stripped from a Walkman, cradled in a bent-up chow spork, connected to a guitar string threaded through the empty Bic. Just as good as anything on the outside. It only takes more time. We may not have much in here, but we've got plenty of time.

I had to blow out the clogged Bic barrel four times before I'd even finished the outline of Homer's bogus number. Slim had come back by then and we all smoked. He told me the new guy's name. Ten months ago Maurice and a friend had been in a '78 Lincoln Continental transformed into a mobile drug lab cooking small batches of some new shit Slim could barely pronounce. It was flammable, of course, and between that and the propane stove they used, soon enough that Lincoln turned into an inferno. Mo had been taking a piss outside the door. His friend was in the backseat, dead.

"Burned while pissing," I said, watching smoke rise from the end of my cigarette. Every time I smoked now I felt a pang of sadness. I tried to memorize every part of the experience, like a loved one I knew was going away. I focused on those thin, silky gray curves I'd never see again.

"Yeah. His forehead nearly melted off. And now he has seizures." Slim took a deep drag then blew the smoke toward the exhaust vent above the stainless-steel toilet. "He said the blast cooked part of his brain."

"What?"

"He takes some drug." Slim yelled out into the hall, "Yo, Maurice, what's that stuff you take?"

"Depakote," came the answer.

The world of prison is upside down. Someone who had blown up his car while cooking drugs would probably be an outcast even in today's shallow, do-nothing-and-become-famous culture, but in prison that guy will be someone of stature. Especially a high-profile case like Maurice's. If your case makes the news, you're a minor celebrity in here, an Arsenio Hall or Jon Lovitz.

It was nearly dinner and I had already smoked the ten cigarettes I allowed myself. I rolled two more for the night along with the ten for the next day. Maybe tomorrow I'd do better.

I'd been sleeping in later and later—mostly because it was a good way to keep from smoking. I woke from a dream where I was in the backseat of an old car, and in the front two men kept cooking something, filling bag after bag of tobacco, handing them back to me, where I hid them in my pants. I was only half awake when our cell door suddenly rolled shut, then all forty-four down the rock clanged shut too. Slim got up and held his mirror outside the bars to see what happened. "Something's going on," he said. "A fight or something."

It was an art, the way he used that mirror. An average person couldn't possibly do it—the slightest flick of the wrist moved the view out of the frame. You have to have a very steady hand, and even then it's still tricky, like bringing in a distant TV station with the old rabbit ears antenna; it never came in perfectly, except by accident.

It was more than a fight, though, more than some smoker's debt catching up to him. We didn't know it until Pete, Maurice's bunkie, was sent back early from his maintenance job. A gray-haired white man named Butch had apparently "beaten the brakes off" a CO named Lodge. It seemed strange to me—Lodge was smart and quiet, unlike the typical COs, who tended to be loud rednecks, unemployable anywhere else. When I thought of Lodge I thought only of the dry skin condition he had—flakes of dandruff coated the shoulders of his uniform like light dust. Butch had not only beaten him up, but was in the process of cracking his skull on the concrete floor like a hard-boiled egg when he was Tasered. "The whole place is locked down," said Pete. "There's blood all over the telephone room floor."

The doors didn't open again for two days. No one went anywhere, except kitchen workers who brought us our food in paper bags. Lodge didn't die, but Channel 8 out of Grand Rapids said he had head injuries and would remain in the hospital under observation for at least another day. As further punishment, we all knew what was coming: our cells would be tossed, we just didn't know when. I took apart my tattoo gun and stuck the motor back in the shell of the cassette player. I flushed the guitar-string needles and the ink-stained barrel of the Bic. And then we waited.

I expected the television to be turned off next. Though we pay for luxuries like cable through the Prisoner Benefit Fund, in the end it's all controlled by the warden. Sure enough, that afternoon during a *Sanford and Son* marathon, the screen went blank. I turned it off and leafed through a tattoo magazine. On the bunk below me, I heard Slim unscrew the cable on his television to maybe pick up a local station via his antenna made from a headphone wire. "PBS," he said after a few minutes. "That's something, anyway."

Slim liked to talk about which era he would live in if given the choice. It was his go-to subject when he thought something needed to be said. Some people see silence as a space they're responsible for filling, and Slim was one of those people. He had a salesman's gift for talking, probably could have been a hell of a car salesman, had he not trained his talent on selling heroin.

His favorite era, I think, the one he talked about most anyway, was the prehistoric era, when dinosaurs ruled the Earth. He wasn't bothered by any logic in these daydreams—it made no difference that humans didn't actually walk the planet back then, but he talked a lot about training the dinosaurs like horses and oxen, making the planet into his personal Eden, where he would grow crops and work on populating the world with a vast stable of Cro-Magnon wives.

This time he was talking about Bonnie and Clyde. "You know anything about them?" he said.

"A little," I said. "I've seen the movie."

"It was on last night," he said. "I'd like to live when they lived, but not for the reason you'd think—not robbing banks and road trips and not getting caught or nothing. You know why?"

I didn't.

"Because bras hadn't been invented yet. All those women back then, they just flopped around. You think back then the women were all straitlaced, you know? But they were braless. And that Bonnie, she was a hot little number. Crazy."

I knew he was thinking of Faye Dunaway. I couldn't remember seeing a picture of the real Bonnie Parker, but I was certain she was no braless Faye Dunaway. It was a waste of breath to point out the problems in his fantasies, so I mostly tuned him out, went to my own dreams of the time I'd like to live in: the future. It was the only era that made sense to me. I knew all too much about the past. The past was the past, and all of it, as far as I was concerned, was a nightmare, nothing worth thinking about. But the future—there was hope in the future, there was the chance that things could be new and different.

A whole platoon of COs walked to the end of our hall, walkie-talkies squawking and chirping like robot birds. They emptied the last ten cells, led the inmates off somewhere, and began searching. They carried portable metal detectors and long sticks with mirrors on the end to look under and above everything. After fifteen minutes the first inmates were brought back, and the next ten, us, were led to B-Ward—an indoor gym area with tables and weight-lifting equipment.

It was my first real look at Maurice. The four of us sat around a table. He'd had a previous year most people couldn't even imagine, thinking he was probably dead, hearing his friend burn to death, finding himself in prison for forty to sixty, essentially the rest of his life. I thought I could feel sedate pain permeating his every movement. He didn't shift a hand from one spot of the table to another without thinking about it, as if he was afraid any move he made might lead to tragedy. He listened and smiled at Slim, holding forth on the braless women of the 1920s. Pete, Maurice's bunkie, said Slim was full of shit. He said women had been wearing bras since the time of Columbus. "Isn't that right, Mo?"

"I never gave it much thought," he said.

"He's no expert on the history of bras—and you sure as hell ain't either," said Slim. "I doubt you've even seen a bra."

A couple of COs came through the door and one of them said, "Jenkins." Mo stood up and walked over to them, showed them his ID, and then they put the cuffs on behind his back, leading him off.

"What the hell?" Pete asked us. "He never did anything but write some letters."

I figured that was the last time I would ever see Mo. In my twenty years I had seen men, here one minute and gone an instant later, moved to one of Michigan's forty different prisons. Some of those men I was happy never to see again, but not Mo. I had felt something around him—he was so fresh out of the oven of tragedy that he had something indefinable about him, some knowledge of another world. He was led out, and I silently wished him well.

When we returned to our cells, our thin blue-green mattresses were on the floor and there were papers everywhere. The Walkman where I kept my tattoo motor was gone. I had left it in plain sight on the table next to the door. There was no sense trying to hide it—I thought if I left it out in the open it wouldn't look suspicious. But it was gone. I had bought it years ago for a bag of coffee.

I started picking up the scattered little squares of card stock that I'd turned into business cards:

PRISON INK
by Ollie Peacock
slinging ink and painting cards
since 1990

Slim was carrying on about some colored pencils that he couldn't find. I had bigger problems. Without tattoos, there was no way to come up with the money I owed. My sight went dark for a second. I felt dizzy. I wanted to beat the shit out of that stupid bastard Butch for starting all of this. I wanted to beat the shit out of the COs that had taken my Walkman. I wanted to strangle the prick who had come up with the idea of removing tobacco from the prisons. Mostly though, I just wanted my motor back. I was on my hands and knees collecting these cards with my name on them, wishing I could just as easily put my life back together.

"I would like to live during Prohibition," Slim said.

"That doesn't make any damn sense," I said. "Why would you want to live without alcohol?"

"That's why—I'd make my own and be a gangster."

"Do you even know how?"

The rock was quiet. It was nearly dinner and the cell searches had been over for hours. I explained to Slim what little I knew about fermentation and distillation. He listened quietly, asking questions now and then. I felt guilty—which happened every time I got tired of his dreams and interjected some reality. He would get quiet, almost submissive, and I would feel as if I had scolded a child or a shy puppy.

We were brought brown-bag dinners of bologna and cheese sandwiches, carrot sticks, and an oatmeal cookie. Someone yelled that the TVs were back on. It was a relief. As I switched channels I saw Mo pass, his bandaged head a white streak out the corner of my eye. "What happened?" I said.

"I was dumb," he said. "I'd drawn a map to a friend, letting her know where I was. I didn't even think."

Mo had a friend from Kalamazoo, he said, a woman

named Lorna who wrote him once a month. He had drawn a detailed map of the Michigan Reformatory—the yard, with its concrete benches, the line of phones and the basketball courts, the chapel and the chow hall, the gym and the gun towers, the ribbons of razor wire atop the fences, the octagonal rotunda, even the abandoned backstop from the baseball diamond that hadn't seen action in twenty years—all culminating in a little *x* on the top bunk in 29.

He had stuck the map in a file folder until he could get some envelopes. The way he described the map, the time and details he'd invested in it, he wanted Lorna to know exactly where he was—literally, of course, but also in a deeper, unspoken way. His map, whether he realized it or not, was a love letter in code. He had spent hours on the details, and the long odds of the two of them ever getting together didn't matter. It was just the idea of her knowing where he was. A sliver of hope in that knowing. The COs, of course, thought of it as escape plans.

"What'd you plead?" Slim asked.

"Stupidity," he said. "I told them the truth."

Slim looked at him with disgust, as if Mo had just said he was a pedophile. He couldn't even consider that the truth was something a person might consider telling. Mo's door opened. "They found me not guilty," he said.

•

After a week of bag lunches, they let us walk down to the chow hall. The hallways were ankle-deep with trash, the windows spotted with wads of wet toilet paper that had dried to a gray plaster. It was the standard result of a prolonged lockdown. When the porters had tried to clean the mess they had been pelted with insults and AA batteries, until the staff stopped sending them into the line of fire.

Other than chow, we weren't allowed to go outside for yard until the second week of December. Besides being opened briefly to let us out for chow, the doors were closed at all times. Some legal-beagle inmates, who spent their time in the law library trying to convince themselves the answers were there, were all in an uproar about the prison taking away our constitutional rights without due process. Others said that we had no rights to open cell doors at all, so they hadn't taken anything away. No one was happy, that was for sure.

I was drawing out possible tattoos for Mo, even though he knew I didn't have a motor anymore. "Well, when you get one," he'd said, "I want a flower or heart, something for the friends and family I've lost." It was the day of the last commissary when we could still buy tobacco, and Mo gave me his pouch of Bugler. He didn't smoke.

"I don't know, Mo," I said, as I had already planned on not paying my tobacco bill and was considering doing exactly what Doo-Wop had done. I couldn't tell anyone, of course, but I couldn't refuse Mo's pouch of Bugler either. I figured I'd smoke like a king until the last and after that, I didn't know.

The next day, via messages passed up and down the

blocks, the inmates had agreed to protest our lockdown by picking up our chow trays like usual, then walking directly to the window near the exit and handing the untouched food to the dishwasher. It was a civilly disobedient act, but anything out of the norm could be considered inciting a riot, and then all bets were off. We'd enter a different dimension of prison life from there. This was no college campus sit-in. This was the real deal. And in a society where the warden was tasked with not losing control, that came with a nearly unlimited amount of power, including deadly force.

The blocks were released half at a time. It was a pretty low-impact protest, yet by the time I picked up my tray, I was nervous. Where generally chow was a hundred men or more sitting four to a table eating, there were maybe a dozen in the entire room. I walked past my usual seat and set the tray on the shelf for the porter to dump it all into the trash. It was a small act but I felt a rush of adrenaline all the same.

There was a space between us all, a chasm separating the men who had eaten their tacos and beans and those of us who hadn't. They had their excuses: They were getting paroled soon. They were too hungry. They couldn't get another misconduct ticket. There are always excuses, but what it really came down to was fear. I did it. Mo did it. Slim and Pete did not, and if the nonprotesters fit any sort of common profile, it was this: the biggest talkers, the ones who could go on and on about who was full of shit, how crappy the food was, how inhumane the cells were—they were the ones who were afraid. It was hard for me to feel too superior though, knowing that my future included skipping out on my debt with a trip to the hole.

The next day everyone ate lunch and dinner as usual. There were twice as many COs in the chow hall, all packing Tasers, and many looked disappointed that we were behaved. They were no doubt jacked up from the powwow with the warden they had at the start of their shift. The Tasers, bright yellow and black striped like a bumblebee, fit snugly in plastic holders attached to their belts. All of them kept a hand at their hip, ready for action that, at least that day, never came.

Mo and I walked outside the chow hall. A man named Tony caught up with me on the sidewalk. I had never said more than two words to Tony before, so I knew what it was about. "You owe a lot," he said. "Some people want to know, the fuck you plan to do?" He was from Sweden or Norway—someplace cold like that, had been down for over thirty years. He had an accent and could hardly say a sentence without a few *fuck*s thrown in.

"I'm good," I said. "Next store. Plus I just got a new motor and a lot of tattoos lined up."

"How about you give them something right now, so you won't fucking lock up? Your TV, maybe."

We walked slowly toward the cellblocks. It was December—cold, but the sun was out, bright and crisp. "No," I said. Mo was walking to my left, his hand on the bandage on his head as if it was suddenly hurting. I could feel him moving away from us. "I don't owe you anything, Tony. I don't even know why you're involved."

"I'm like a fucking bank," he said. "Sometimes a bank will, you know, consolidate loans and make some fucking money on the payment." He twisted a Velcro-banded watch around his wrist, then smiled slightly. "I know you're good. Next store, huh?" He spit on the sidewalk, as if it was the official end to what he had to say, then caught up with a group of guys—nonsmoking thugs, no doubt.

"What's his deal?" Mo asked.

"You're just lucky you don't smoke," I said. "I should have fucking punched him. I'd be out of this whole deal, on my way to the hole."

"It's that easy, huh?"

"Not really," I said. "I'd be in the hole for a while, but they'd probably put me right back here."

"You got the money to pay them?"

"No."

"That's all right, man. We've all got secrets. I don't really have seizures either. I just like the Depakote. They give me Tegretol, too, but I sell those. Some guys like to snort them. Soon as I heard they give out meds, I got the idea to fall down and shake like a poisoned rat. I do that every now and then and nobody asks any questions. Sometimes I'll slip half an Alka-Seltzer in my mouth and spit foam everywhere."

We walked up the stairs in I-Block, up to the third floor, then down the hall to the cells. I asked him how badly he had been burned.

"I need a couple more skin grafts. It basically burned off half of my head. We were using naphtha on a Coleman stove and when it went up, it was like the inside of that Lincoln was napalmed. It burned for a long time. You think time in prison is slow, try setting yourself on fire, then see how slow time passes."

Everyone was back in their cells, but Mo and I stood talking through the bars. He said he couldn't explain what it was like in that Lincoln when it all went to hell and his friend was in the back, screaming, and all he could do was flop out onto the parking lot and try to put himself out. Worse than his friend screaming was when the firemen pulled the body out while the paramedics went about stabilizing Mo. What was left was steaming, shrunken, and charred like a log from a doused bonfire.

He had been charged with negligent homicide and about a dozen drug charges and danger to society felonies. He denied responsibility for the death, though. His friend had been aware of the risk. This may have been true, but in the end, it was only an excuse. I didn't try to argue with him, get him to see how he may have been just a little responsible for the trouble he found himself in. Just like everyone else in here, he had a right to be wrong. He would change, or he wouldn't. Some men never do. They spend the rest of their lives denying the truth, protecting the illusions that protect them from their past.

The two of us just stood there awhile. It is hard to explain what standing near Mo felt like to me. He had a kind of knowledge no one really wants to come by honestly, because it involves unimaginable loss. He had literally been to hell and back, and part of him knew it. Someone like that—someone who has had layers burned away to reveal something essential—is worth knowing.

The laundry porters began handing back our clean clothes in our laundry bags. They were whispering to everyone that tomorrow afternoon's yard was going to be a silent protest. We were going to walk around and around the track in a group very slowly. I didn't really understand the point, but we would at least let them know we could push back. We hadn't done anything wrong, yet were being punished as if we had. And all this time, the idiot who *had* done something wrong wasn't even here any longer.

Word got around that about half of the men—Slim and Pete included—weren't going to do anything but stay in their cells during the afternoon yard. I was going, of course. I didn't know how it would play out, but I figured I could be on my way out of here somehow. I picked up my little stack of business cards, reached around the cell, and set them on the flat, horizontal slats outside Mo's door. "Mo," I said. "Keep these. Maybe I'll see you again."

"I'm sure you will," he said. Though he seemed to know tomorrow would be it for me, he didn't seem to understand that we probably would never see each other again. I'd been around long enough to know better—when someone was gone, they were gone for good.

It hadn't snowed at all in Michigan that winter, except for a few flurries around Thanksgiving. But it snowed that night, all night, as I sat by the window rolling the last of my tobacco. When I thought about it, I would miss rolling cigarettes most of all. Maybe more than the actual smoking. There was something in the ritual of it, the shredding of the long strands into smaller pieces, and that smell—the damp grass and the freshly plowed field—it was soothing and slow, a throwback to a simpler time, with simpler pleasures.

I smoked in relative silence. Slim talked a little bit in his sleep, and I could hear Mo snoring in the next cell. I watched the fat snowflakes fall through the brightness of the lights outside. I smoked the cigarettes as far down as I could, often singeing the ends of my fingers, an easier pain, I thought, than the pain of quitting. I wanted it to hurt, that way it would be easier to remember.

Only a hundred of us went out to the yard that day. Usually there were three times that. We all just gathered in a loose group—like those strange flocks of birds that come together and become one—and we walked very slowly around the quarter-mile asphalt track. There was much whispering going on above the soft rustle of our state-issued shoes on the blacktop.

The large yard is an acre of flat ground set outward from the two five-story cellblocks. There were a dozen or so concrete benches on the edge of the track and five chin-up bars, two basketball courts, and opposite those, two dozen phones. There were tables, too, where men played cards and dominoes and were warned via stenciled messages on the tabletops not to sit on the actual table or to stand anywhere around them.

After we'd been walking for ten minutes, two more men with guns appeared on the roof of the blocks. A tall captain in a black, knee-length MDOC coat came out and walked beside the group. "Look," he said, "I know we've got things we need to talk about, and we will, but you guys need to disperse. We'll work something out." No one said anything, though, because no one knew anything. We didn't have a spokesman or a list of demands.

The captain went back into the building and four more men with guns appeared on the roof, one of them with a large-bore shotgun. A new guard on the ground had a bolt of zip-tie handcuffs strapped across his chest like a bandolier. Mo walked next to me silently. All of the guns made me nervous. A long line of COs began spacing themselves on the ground about twenty feet outside the bordering fence, the bright yellow of their Tasers glowing against the drab gray of their uniforms.

And then she was there. The warden, who someone had said was on vacation, had apparently been called in. She was a fifty-something black woman dressed more for spring than winter in an aqua-colored sundress and matching blue pumps. She was a classy lady I'd seen around a few times. Today, though, she had her left arm in a sling. Her fingers stuck out of the end and looked swollen the closer she got to us—like large, spoiling sausages.

Just outside the yard, there was a brick, octagonal chapel with a tall, nondenominational, steeple-like structure on top, and past that, a long, fading white brick wall. Five armed guards now stood on top of that wall.

The warden walked briskly to the group as we passed through the shadow of J-Block. She stood, flanked by four COs, to the side of us. "I'm giving you one warning," she said. "Break up." We kept walking, and when we made it back around to the shadowed area ten minutes later, she began demanding men's prison IDs, and the guys in front reached into their pockets to comply.

Mo elbowed me. "Showtime," he whispered, then popped something white into his mouth. He stepped out of the crowd and fell to the ground, shaking violently on his stomach. Everyone backed away and a CO kneeled down and shifted him onto his back, and I could see the sizzling foam around Mo's lips. Before anyone knew what was happening, before I even knew what I was doing, I took two steps and reached down to the yellow and black stripes at the CO's belt, ripping the Taser right out of his holster.

I leveled it at the warden and squeezed. There was a kick, like that of a handgun, as the tiny explosive launched the sharp probes. I saw the warden freeze, eyes skyward, and drop like a dead tree to the cold ground just before I did the same, stuck by several of those same electric fires in my back. It was like lightning passing throughout my body. It seemed to last forever the way it traveled down my hands, reaching through my fingertips, the current running through me, trying to find its way out.

BROTHER GOOSE

A kid told me, as we walked the small yard of Level 4, that he saw a bird land on razor wire once, causing its feet to bleed. The stuff is *that* sharp, he said. It isn't true, of course. I see sparrows land on the sharp edges often, though I can't see them do it now without imagining their tiny claws with surgically precise injuries, the width of paper cuts.

Razor wire is like Slinkys for masochistic giants that sit atop every fence, doubled up on buildings and the ground. It's sometimes called "concertina." I don't know why. That sounds like a twenty-dollar cocktail at Lincoln Center before the Prokofiev premiere—the opposite of what we are supposed to believe this stuff will do to flesh.

I have seen plastic bottles and empty coffee bags impaled permanently on the regularly spaced spikes that are meant to snag the clothing of anyone intent on slinking through. The containers remain there, empty—warning flags fading and flapping over the years.

At a prison in Muskegon, a man decided to slink out.

It was the middle of the day, and even if he had gotten through, he was nowhere near an actual exit, though to the law there wouldn't be any difference. Attempted escape to nowhere will still get you five more years. There was new snow on the ground. I didn't see the actual attempt, but I saw his handcuffed hands as they brought him past some of us gathered, smoking, and they dripped a constant red trail across the white sidewalk, as if marking the way back home in some dark fairy tale. The trail disappeared in minutes under new snow.

At a neighboring prison, two men hijacked a garbage truck using homemade pepper spray and tried driving through the fence, but the wire got ahold of one man's clothes, shredding his arm like red cabbage for coleslaw. The longer some are here, the more they believe that there are ways around that ribbony razorness. If the person is thin enough and lithe enough, can he not slip through the football-shape space of the extended wire—which, incidentally, is more like the thin ribbons trailing the handlebars of childhood bicycles than wire? Or wrap himself in cardboard and layers of clothing as a shield. The wire is only sharp if you touch it, and the longer some study it, the more they believe it won't touch them.

But what is the goose's excuse? He came from the outside in. One minute he was grazing casually with his southward-traveling gaggle on the grassy hill across the road, and the next lying partially shaved on the yard, flapping, spraying goose blood.

I was on top of my bunk, after dinner. I thought that maybe one of the greyhounds in the prison dog program—as fast as horses—had broken free of her handler with the leash and run the goose down. Then I saw an inmate in the cautious circle around the injured bird point to a downy remnant snagged like an old pillow on the wire. The goose would flap, turning in a tight circle, then quit, the circle of men widening and then closing in again. In a few minutes, he lay still. A CO brought a large gray Inedible barrel from the kitchen, and an inmate picked the bird up by his feet, dropping him in. Then he wiped his hands on a nearby patch of grass.

For days afterward, the passing dogs were drawn to the bloody grass like metal to a magnet, until a good cold rain washed it all away.

The geese on the hill are gone now, down south where it's warm. They talk quietly to one another about the gander they lost, who thought he could make it through, who didn't believe what everyone had told him about the razor wire. There's always one, they probably say, shaking their heads in sympathetic disbelief. There is always one. And then they shiver slightly—though it's warm out—remembering the sound their brother made as he bled to death in that other world.

ENGULFED

When fucked-up people end up inside they can be whoever they want. A crackhead becomes a former high-class pimp. A tax evader was a master forger and poker champ. There are PGA golfers and NASCAR drivers, CEOs, billiards pros, and drug kingpins who were probably only street-level pushers. There was a pedophile who said he used to be a porn star named Double Deuce Domino. A lot of them were rich—some from old family money, some won the lottery. And not just a few thousand from the scratch-offs, but Powerball millions. One man swore Perry Mason was his old attorney, and it was his case that made him famous enough to land the TV show. It goes on and on: war heroes, doctors, authors, rock stars, a lot of jet-setting playboys, a man who said he wrote several episodes of *Seinfeld* though he was barely smart enough to tie his own shoes.

This is who I was. On the outside, I'd focus on a neighborhood for a month, breaking into a few houses, causing a localized panic, then I'd go around selling phony home security contracts. This is how I learned to lie, how I learned to live in a world made by the mind—not a life *of* the mind, but *by* the mind. The way God did it.

A lie is in the details. It's in the American-made midsize rental car with the magnetic "Max Steele Security" sign stuck to the door. It's in the khaki slacks, the knit polo shirts with the embroidered "MSS" above the heart, and the ostrich-skin Dunhill briefcase I stole from a home outside of Philly. It was in the three levels of security systems I offered, and in the white granite Montblanc pen I put in each quivering, homeowning hand to sign the check for the deposit and the first month's fees.

Most people on the outside are liars too. They slept with umpteen women before they were eighteen, they were homecoming queen, they were accepted to the Ivy League but decided against it. They say things were better way back when. They say they'll love you forever. They go to a bank and buy whole lives they can't afford. The entire economy is part of a world of lies, and prison is just a city in that world. A city of lies.

Our cells were two-man and I'd had the same bunkie for a year. His name was Tim and he liked to gamble. But when he got too far in, when he owed too much to the wrong people, he "locked up," which means he wrote a letter to a CO saying he was in fear for his life. If you write it, they have to believe it. So they put him in protective custody, eventually moving him to another joint. I still miss Tim.

Then there was Richard, who shaved his head every day. He'd been here just forty-eight hours and we were in the lunch line awaiting fish. The chow hall smelled like high tide. He turned around and said, "The air tastes funny," then dropped dead right there. What could we do? We all went ahead and ate.

Malcolm was next. A dead ringer for a young Charles Manson. Somebody split his head open with a sock full of batteries because he tried to steal someone's boyfriend.

Jo July lasted a week before he made an assaultive comment to a large, female staffer. He cornered her outside the staff restroom, asked if he could go in and take a deep whiff of the toilet seat she'd just sat on.

Brian moved in an hour after Jo left. For a week he said absolutely nothing, then one day he sat calmly at the desk and began eating envelopes until the inside of his mouth was pasty and bloody. So they shipped him to Huron Valley, where the bugs go.

Robert was next. I didn't even talk to him for a couple of days because I figured, What's the point? He didn't need me to talk anyway. He talked enough on his own, which was remarkable because he had a terrible stutter, beginning every sentence with "I mean I mean I mean, um, um, um . . ." He would say the same thing in the middle and again at the end. The simplest idea would take him five minutes to express. This did not stop him from talking, nor did the perpetual piece of E. Z. Digby's butterscotch candy he'd keep in his mouth, rattling like a rock tumbler. I don't know what was worse: having to wait through the stuttering, or all that wet smacking on the E. Z. Digby's.

I kept expecting him to disappear—his stuff, his bedding, the box full of Bic pens he used to write to his six women. I kept expecting him to be gone when I got back from lunch, or work, even a shower. But he stayed. On his bulletin board he put up pictures of women he said were old and current girlfriends: thin, blond, angelic-looking women, and then their polar opposites—dark-haired stripper types flashing black panties from atop custom Harleys. In the middle of this lineup of sluts and angels were the pictures of his house and Hummer.

"That's, I mean I mean I mean, um, um, um, my house," he said. It was a perfectly landscaped, red-brick ranch—a charming suburban dream home. There were a couple of interior pictures, like the big, beautiful fireplace, with a line of twenty Hummel figurines on the mahogany mantel. They looked like actual German children, frozen, shrunk, and set in radiant porcelain, more human than actual flesh. The fire crackled below them and made the brown leather furniture glisten so brightly I could smell it.

Then the garage, with a tall cabinet of Snap-on tools behind that brand-new champagne-colored Hummer. Altogether the pictures must have depicted about eight hundred grand worth of home, property, and vehicle. Altogether it was a horrible lie. Unbelievable to the utmost.

Robert was tattooed in twenty years' worth of fading prison ink that represented the iconic logos and designer names of a millionaire's lifestyle: Mercedes, Gucci, Armani, Ferrari, Rolex, and about twenty more. He thought he had expensive taste, but he had never actually owned anything represented by these names. He wouldn't know Dom Pérignon from Dom DeLuise. He had never been on the inside of a Hummer; he didn't know any of those women and probably hadn't even seen any like them in real life. He had names for them, sure, but that was it—if pressed, he would know nothing about them. Robert was an amateur. He assumed that just because he desired something, that made it real enough. What he didn't know was that even in here, you have to work for it.

I studied Robert for a full month, writing down all the lies that made it around that little piece of E. Z. Digby's. It seemed the less I talked, the more he tried to impress me. I think the only word I said to him that entire month was "Really?"

After thirty days I had a list of 152 lies. Here's a partial list, edited to take out the stuttering and the wet smacks on his butterscotch:

He punched a female warden twice.
His ex-wife was once a centerfold in *Penthouse.*
His father was a submarine captain who was lost at sea.

Geronimo was a relative (also: Timothy McVeigh, Babe Ruth, Abraham Lincoln, and many more, usually whoever was on the History Channel recently).

Julia Roberts was a pen pal.

A famous director (he couldn't remember his name) almost made a movie about him. I suggested some possible names, and he thought Robert Altman sounded right.

His brother is seven three.

His brother is an attorney who has never lost a case.

He owned four tattoo parlors—which is actually somewhat believable because he did decent tattoos. Still, I kept it on my list. I mean, four?

He used to make heroin from an acre of homegrown poppies and a recipe handed down from Genghis Khan (recently featured on the History Channel).

He died twice and met God both times.

He's bungee-jumped, parachuted, hot-air-ballooned, and flown an F-15 (plus the stories of near-fatal mishaps involving all of them).

There was a gorgeous call girl who used to pay him for sex.

He made a prison bomb out of his color TV, which is why we could only have black-and-white sets.

He murdered a pedophile bunkie, disposing of his body with a Bic razor and his cell's toilet.

He used law-enforcement-grade pepper spray to spice up his pizza.

He was in a coma for a year and a half. He woke up
with a nurse humping him.

You get the idea. Whatever Robert wanted to have done, whomever he wanted to have been, whomever he wanted to have known, screwed, or been a relative of, it all suddenly was. He knew nothing of the restraint it took to stay believable, or the care required to make something real. He simply floated from one idea to the next, completely unmoored, chomping on his yellow, fragrant candy.

The woman I fell in love with, the woman in the neighborhood on the outskirts of Portland, Oregon, had a collection of more than fifty Hummel figurines worth around $18,000. They were kept behind glass doors on four rows of recessed shelves above her dining room table. They were so bright and clean that their reflections shone off the dark polished wood like photographed images of ghosts. Having seen real Hummels, I could spot them anywhere, even in a picture of someone's make-believe fireplace mantel.

I spent a long time staring at them, imagining their perfect, stationary lives. They were Alpine youth happily engaged in chores and games from a simpler time: a girl jumping rope (the "rope" held the girl aloft, forever defying gravity); a boy in lederhosen led a sheep with his staff; another boy aimed a slingshot skyward; a girl with long, blond pigtails kicked a yellow ball. Each of them seemed frozen with personalities as unique as living beings. My favorite was a mischievous little girl lighting the fuse of a waist-high bottle rocket.

I loved the woman, of course, but when I think of her now, I think just as much of the twenty-eight boys and thirty little girls in soothing rows on the wall of her dining room. It even takes a moment for me to remember her name, Mary, but I can picture the fifty-eight little faces with no trouble at all.

Like a pro taking pity on a hopeless amateur, I decided I would teach Robert some lessons of the lie. He was writing letters, and every five minutes or so he'd look through the horizontal bars out the window. The weather was changing, and the first official day of spring was only a few days away. There were melting piles of snow outside, shrinking a little bit every day like distant, white mountains diminishing in a time-lapse video.

Robert was going to get back into shape pretty soon, he said. He was going to get back into weight lifting, and then he told me what good shape he used to be in. "I mean I mean I mean, I could do like a hundred um, um, um, push-ups. Um, without breathing."

"My boxing coach told us push-ups were the best exercise you can ever do," I told him. "Especially when you hold them at the bottom and count to twenty. My coach was an old black guy. You know anything about boxing, Robert?"

"Um um um, yeah."

"Then maybe you've heard of him: 'Coffee Machine' Mitchell. He fought Thomas 'The Hit Man' Hearns once in Detroit. Coffee Machine was pro for a few years."

"I mean I mean I mean, yeah, I saw that fight. Um um um, I remember that fight."

"No you don't, Robert. No you didn't."

He looked at me blankly and then down at his faded, tattooed arms, as if there were some answer there. I felt sorry for him, but he had to learn. And learning is often a painful process.

"I made all of that up. There's no Coffee Machine Mitchell, and I've done about fifty push-ups in my entire life. I think you've probably done about the same."

I'd be lying if I said I wasn't worried in that moment. Robert was bigger than me, and I didn't know anything about fighting. It was risky. It was a gamble. The door was shut and if he wanted to, he could lay down a serious beating on me before a guard could come with a key.

What I'd done was called him a liar, which was serious. Once you become a number, all you are is the words you use. If your words aren't real, then neither are you. Being called a liar to your face was just a notch above "snitch." But I had learned enough about criminals to know someone who regularly advertised how bad he was at something subconsciously wanted to get caught. Robert wanted my help, I could tell.

He didn't say anything for a while after that. It was the quietest he'd been since he had moved in. It was entirely possible that he couldn't speak. Finally, after about ten minutes, when it was obvious I was out of physical danger, I broke the silence. "Do you know what made that a good lie?"

"Um um um," he said, "I believed it. I mean I mean I mean, I never thought it was a lie."

"If I had said Muhammad Ali coached me, or Sugar Ray Leonard or something, it isn't believable. It's too much, Robert. Though one time I did almost sell Sugar Ray Leonard an alarm system for his new garage. But his wife said they didn't need another alarm because the perimeter was guarded. And his daughter, talk about a knockout."

"Um um um, that's pretty cool. Leonard, huh?" He opened up another butterscotch, and as he handed one to me I saw the spark in his eyes die again. "Um um um, you just made that up, didn't you?"

"I like you, Robert. And if you want help, I'll help you." I lit up a cigarette and pointed at his bulletin board. "That's not your house, those aren't your ex's Hummels, that's not your Hummer, and none of those women are your girlfriends. I've got to tell you—no one here believes a word you say. So let's start over. Let's reset things. How about you don't say another word for twenty-four hours."

He started to say something, then stopped himself. He was probably going to defend his wall of pictures, his world of lies. But he didn't. He looked out the window at the vanishing piles of snow.

Mary already had an alarm system. I think it was ADT, maybe Brinks, but I stopped by anyway because I always made a point to meet every person in the neighborhood I was working. She invited me in, coffee already brewing. She'd heard of me through the neighborhood grapevine. She had pastel Easter basket earrings dangling from her ears, though it was September.

"I see you're all set on alarms. You haven't been broken into recently, I'll bet." Of course I knew she hadn't—it was good business to steer clear of alarmed houses. It only strengthened my sales at unalarmed places.

"No, I haven't," she said. "But that's okay. I'll get you some coffee." She went into the kitchen. I heard coffee cups rattle and the closing of cabinet doors. "I've had an alarm for a long time. Come in here and I'll show you."

I figured she was going to show me the activation sequence pad, which meant I'd have to say something like "Yeah, the 143-Z, that's a good system." You always compliment the competition. But she led me into the dining room instead, where she flipped on the track lights over her shelves.

"I had to protect these," she said, handing me a full cup. "They're Hummels."

"They're beautiful," I said. And they were. I could smell the mountains where they lived. I could hear their small, innocent voices telling me to stay awhile, telling me Mary would make a very nice companion.

I sat with her in the dining room, looking out of a picture window at three soft volcanoes the color of orange sherbet from the setting sun. We talked mostly about the Hummels, how some were her grandmother's from sixty years ago. She said it was almost like adopting children—the effort that went into deciding which one to buy next.

Every half hour the snow on the volcanoes changed colors. They were purple when she told me she was a set designer. "You mean like plays?" I asked, and she said only occasionally. She mostly built sets for Portland State University's forensics department. She spent weeks outfitting rooms or entire houses, only to have professional arson investigators come up with creative ways to set them on fire. Burn units, she called them. One was "going up" tomorrow. "They're burning it," she said. "You busy?"

I told her I wasn't.

She was pretty, bright, and animated talking about her job. She was fairly old though that hardly matters. It made her more attractive somehow—she knew exactly who she was. She didn't try to cover up her thin face with makeup, which revealed a pale smartness about her eyes that made up for anything she might have lacked. She wore white painter's pants splattered with colorful drips and a Western button-down shirt with vertical strands of silver thread that sparkled when light hit it a certain way. Her long, brown hair wasn't styled so much as restrained in a complex arrangement of bobby pins and elastic ponytail holders.

I looked up at the shelves of Hummels. I didn't know what the word meant, but I thought maybe it was German for "frozen happiness." Not all of them were smiling, but you could tell they were very content, if only for that moment.

"So you gonna show me your goods?" she asked me.

"My what?"

"Your goods. Your systems. I want to take a look. I've been thinking about something more advanced."

We looked through the brochures for about five minutes. "I'll take plan A," she said. "It's got the carbon-monoxide sensor. I like that."

Plan A was the most comprehensive of my made-up plans, not to mention expensive. "Usually homeowners with children get that one. You know, 'the silent killer' fear."

"Well I don't have any children, but that doesn't mean I deserve to die in my sleep."

"Of course not," I said, handing her my Montblanc.

"Nice pen," she said. She signed the check and the eyes of all those happy children looked past me, as if to look directly on my guilt was impossible.

"Good coffee," I said.

I liked Mary from the start. Maybe I loved her from the start. I don't know—it's a tough call. But I know it wasn't Mary that made me want to live an honest life. It was the Hummels. It was those beautiful, honest little lives under the bright lights in that dining room. My deceitful ways were no match for their purity.

Robert didn't say one word for an entire twenty-four hours. Then he didn't say another word the next day. After the third day, it became pretty obvious he was making a statement.

People started coming up to me, people who used to gather around Robert just for entertainment. His silence, apparently, was less amusing. "Look," I told four or five of them smoking outside our unit's door, "I told him the truth."

"What do you mean you told him the truth?"

"I told him he was a horrible liar."

"Fuck that," said the spokesman of the Robert fan club. "That wasn't your place, man. It may be bad for both of you if he stays quiet. A person can only go about forty days without talking and then they die."

I knew he had talking and eating mixed up, but I was outnumbered. And I understood what he meant by missing the old Robert. His silence was unnerving, and in the company of others, his lies were pretty entertaining. Lies are a drug here; prisoners are addicts and as any addict sinks deeper and deeper into their sickness, they seek out people who are worse off than them so they don't feel so bad about themselves.

When I was extradited from Oregon, then Ohio, then to West Virginia, Pennsylvania, Alabama, New Jersey, then finally here to Michigan to serve a twenty-year concurrent sentence, I found a present waiting for me under my gangrene-colored plastic mattress: a book with the front and back covers ripped off, a retrospective history of *The Beverly Hillbillies.*

In my new home behind bars, I always looked for signs, things I thought of as anchors—sent from the universe to let me know I wasn't forgotten. In a county jail in West Virginia I had found a penny, heads-up, on the floor outside my cell. Some inmates go thirty years without seeing actual money. I took the penny as a good sign and rubbed it with my thumb to a new brightness before flipping it into the wishing well of the toilet the day I headed to Pennsylvania.

In Michigan, I took the book as a similar good sign, and if you had a mind like I did to study that book, you could come away knowing more about that show—which ran from September 26, 1962, until March 23, 1971—than its creator, Paul Henning.

I landed here and latched on to a new life. I could forget about my dismal home by focusing on a fictional one, the real people who made that world. Granny, for example—Irene Ryan—who loved to bet on the ponies and drink Scotch. She sounded like a perfect grandmother.

Donna Douglas, who played Elly May, fell in love with Elvis after working with him on the movie *Frankie and Ricky.* I was touched and drawn to her heartbreak and depression after he rebuffed her. Donna's fictional father, Buddy Ebsen, was born in Belleville, Illinois, just east of St. Louis—which seemed as good a place as any to pretend to be from if I needed to. The book even had recipes for his favorite dishes, Deviled Hawk Eggs, Coot Cobbler, and Hog Jowls Melba.

I didn't know when, where, or how I was going to use the information in that book, but I absorbed it with the belief that it would one day be important to a new life. I hadn't planned on sharing the book with anyone, but after Robert hadn't said a word for a week and a half, I was desperate. I had been in that Michigan cell for several months, reading about that decades-old TV show in the midnight quiet by the light spilling through the vertical window of our cell door from the hallway.

Robert had begun carving figurines from bars of Irish Spring for a "girlfriend" on the outside. He used an array of hollow Bic barrels with customized tips, laid out on his desk on a green washcloth like surgical instruments. The results—angels, from what I could tell—looked pretty good in that green-marbled medium. As he carved I would read aloud from the book I kept hidden under my mattress, where I had found it. I suggested he could pass himself off as the son of Max Baer, Jr. (Jethro), the grandson of the former boxing heavyweight champion of the world, Max Baer, Sr. He swept a snowy, fragrant pile of soap shavings into our trash can, then began a new angel, or whatever they were.

I sat up on my bunk with my back against the wall, thinking about that suggestion after I'd made it. "Don't you see how it all comes back to boxing?" I said. "That must mean it was meant to be." He looked at me with a heavy stare, then quietly dug out a bottle of black shoe polish from his foot locker and began coating his carvings, which apparently weren't angels, but chess pieces. I went back to reading about how Sharon Tate appeared in many episodes, beginning with "Elly Starts to School," on October 16, 1963, five or six years before those psycho Manson hippies got ahold of her.

Mary's deposit check was the third from her neighborhood. I was running out of time.

We drove south on Interstate 5 and I sat in the passenger's seat watching the tall pines blur past, wondering if the rain would stay away long enough to get this fire started. We ended up in a field adjacent to an elementary school named after a locally born former ambassador to Argentina, or so we read on the plaque near the school. The town was called Tualatin, and a sign on the fence read PRIVATE PROPERTY OF P.S.U. We walked a good quarter mile to a huge garage-type structure with thirty-foot-high sliding hangar doors on two sides. Inside, under the tall skeleton of steel beams, was a plain wooden house. There was an air of anticipation, as if a party were about to begin and we were among the first to arrive.

The house smelled new: sawn wood and carpeting, wallpaper glue and paint, but the interior looked straight out of 1975. There was thick, orange shag carpeting, a green vinyl chair, a table lamp with a faded shade, and an old blue couch where a female mannequin lay. On the lamp table was a half-empty bottle of Wild Turkey that Mary said was actually iced tea. An ashtray full of butts sat on the floor by the couch. The black-haired mannequin was dressed in bright green polyester. Mary said, "She's passed out drunk. I named her Suzy. I picture her a barfly." She realigned one of Suzy's socks, stood back, and looked around, as if checking the scene in preparation for guests. "The students show up later, after everything's wet and cold."

Three men walked through the swinging kitchen door. They could have been from 1975 themselves with their practical WASP haircuts and casual clothes. They congratulated Mary on a fine job and one of them asked my opinion of the place. "It looks real. It looks like where I grew up. Even her," I said, pointing to Suzy. "She reminds me of my mother." I felt weird after I said it, as if it were some arson school faux pas, like telling an actor to have a great show. I thought they might feel bad for burning the place with my mother inside it. But I couldn't take it back, and I couldn't think of anything else to say that would make the silence less awkward.

Mary and I stayed out of the way after that. She said this one wasn't going to be an arson—the drunk mannequin was going to set the place on fire with her cigarette. It was an exam equivalent of a trick question, designed to see what the students might come up with. The men checked the sprinkler system above the house and hooked up a hose to a bright yellow fire hydrant. We watched through one of the house's side windows.

One of the men lit a Winston, smoked an inch of it, then placed it strategically deep in the fibers of the carpet by the couch.

The day was gray—in Oregon, most of them are—and the air was damp and every once in a while I had to wipe the mist off my face. But it seemed like a beautiful day. When the smoke began filling the house, Mary took my hand in hers. "I love and hate this part," she said.

Robert and I were watching episode 218, "The Phantom Fifth Floor," where the Clampetts convert the fifth floor of the bank owned by Mr. Drysdale (played by real-life jackass Raymond Bailey, who once took a swing at an ostrich that wouldn't stick to its mark) into multiple businesses. I was lost in the show when Sergeant Baker unlocked the door, told me to grab my ID and to turn around. He cuffed me. Robert kept watching the little black-and-white TV. He began to smile and someone who didn't know him would have thought he was laughing at Jethro's hijinks.

"What the hell is this all about?" I asked.

The sarge slipped on a pair of latex gloves, like he was about to perform surgery. He held my cuffs by the small connecting chain, and with his other hand reached over and lifted the pillow from my bed, revealing what looked to be a small, semiautomatic pistol. Sarge picked it up and held it in his open palm, testing its heft, and I could smell the soap and shoe polish odor it gave off. "Wow,"

I said, because there was nothing else to say. Sometimes deep inside you know that anything you say is going to sound like a lie, no matter how true it is. I had spent so much time working on lies, the truth wouldn't have anything to do with me when I needed it.

"I was just trying to help, Robert," I said.

"Um, um, um, I guess I didn't need no help." He never took his eyes from the TV. "So so so long, Steven."

My hand was warm in hers. Smoke was rising from unseen cracks in the roof. I couldn't see any flames yet, but I knew it was only a matter of time.

There were kids at recess in the back of the school. They waited at the fence's edge and some sat atop the monkey bars. I pretended they were watching us. I pretended we were famous and they were all trying to catch a glimpse so they could tell their moms when they raced in the front door from school, cheeks flushed and out of breath. Our presence would cling to them like smoke. "Guess who I saw," they would say.

The interior began to glow orange. "The woman on the couch would be dead already," Mary said. "It's the smoke. Victims never really burn to death. They just choke."

The outside walls steamed and blistered. I could see wave after wave of heat flowing off the roof, and then all at once, the waves flashed into flame. "I guess you'll be leaving town soon. I wish you wouldn't." She was quiet for a moment. "I feel new," she said, watching the house. She got out a stick of gum from her back pocket and began chewing.

"I may stick around, Mary." She was almost double my age, but I felt much older around her and the fire. She popped her gum and smiled at me.

The couch was going strong now and through the window I could see the mannequin's hair torch and her light brown skin blister. Her clothes were long gone. The window shattered from the heat and I could hear the children cheering even though the flames gave off a blowtorch roar, louder than I ever thought they could be. "I guess I should tell you the truth about something," she said.

Fire does that to people. Look at campfire. Fireplaces too. Maybe we see our own end in the flames and want to clean the slate. Maybe it's easier to confess without looking anybody in the eyes. "Technically," she said, "I'm married. Technically. I haven't seen him in ten years."

Pictures, clocks, ceiling tiles crashed to the floor. Flames poked through the roof, and soon the whole place was ablaze in orange flame and black smoke. Mary said the sprinklers were about to come on, but they were actually high-density, state-of-the-art water delivery nozzles, which soaked the house in a matter of minutes. Black water snaked in little steaming rivers away from the ruin.

"Well, as long as we're telling the truth," I said, "I want you to know I haven't cashed your check . . ."

And I told her I wouldn't. I told her that I would repay her neighbors too, and I explained to her how the Hummels made me rethink everything about my life. She took my confession as well as anyone could, though it definitely broke the spell of the fire. The flames were out but we kept staring at the wet, smoldering char. The only sound was the hiss of the dying heat. "I guess we should go" was all she said. The kids went back into school, and the fire students came out in white jumpsuits, white booties over their shoes. They wore gas masks and you could hear the rasping of the air as it pulled through the filters. They walked past with little briefcases, like they were going to work in some poison office.

I was arrested in my room at the Knights Inn that evening.

I'm an optimist, however, and I believe Mary saved me. I don't dislike her in particular, or women in general. I once knew a kid who dreamed of hurting women most every night. What can I say—some men end up hating women because their mothers were distant or cold, they drank or slept around, whatever. But not me.

I love my mom.

Born Doris Smith on September 26, 1933 (exactly twenty-nine years before the show appeared on prime time), Donna Douglas married Roland Bourgeois her last year at St. Gerard's High School in Baton Rouge, Louisiana. The marriage only lasted five years. Roland isn't my father. I don't know who is for sure, but I tell people it's Elvis.

My mom is most famous, of course, for portraying Elly May on *The Beverly Hillbillies*—the blond bombshell, critter-loving hick from the Ozarks. I love her in that role, but it's not my favorite.

My favorite role of Mom's I've caught a couple times on late-night TV, when they show the old reruns. It's a *Twilight Zone,* and you can barely tell it's her. For most of the episode, her entire head is wrapped up in gauze, after an operation to transform her hideous face.

The doctors unwrap the bandages, and every time I see it, I always expect to be repulsed by what lies beneath. But her face is perfect, stunning, radiant—and still the doctors and nurses turn away, unable to look. Everyone in the hospital, everyone in that world, has the face of a pig. My mom, it turns out, is the monster. She runs through the hospital screaming, and eventually is welcomed into a colony of beautiful freaks. Though by the episode's end, you could tell she's learned something. I'm not sure what, but you'd have to, changing yourself to be beautiful then finding you're the only pretty one in a world of monsters. You'd have to learn something.

LECHE QUEMADA

Clyde was not surprised that she was late picking him up. Melissa was from the West Coast, carefree and unfettered, and had often criticized him for being too midwestern, too hung up on structure and schedule. They used to argue about it constantly until Clyde finally decided that nothing would change her; he just couldn't win. So it was no surprise that he was waiting. The real surprise was that she had waited for him.

It was just after eight in the morning, and he sat on the concrete and wood bench in front of the control center at E. C. Brooks Correctional. He'd been there for over an hour. But how could he be angry when he was free? How could anybody be angry out here? If someone had come up and cracked him in the head with a baseball bat, he probably would have laughed when he woke up. Maybe, he thought, the last twelve years had been worth what he felt at that moment. Few people in the world would ever experience this kind of warmth, this sheer love for life. The bright morning sun was a glowing, orange lozenge, and its rays seemed medicinal, blanketing him with healing warmth. The light in heaven probably felt like this.

Two officers walked toward him across the parking lot. They wore black baseball caps with the word *transportation* stitched in white letters across the front. They wore gray uniforms with pant legs tucked into their black leather boots. They each carried a 9-mm Glock, and the short one carried a Taser. The taller one was finishing a cigarette and talking about a fish his brother-in-law had caught that weekend. "He thought it was a twelve-inch crappie, but after he filleted it, he realized he'd ruined a record-length bluegill."

"He don't know the difference between a crappie and a bluegill?"

"Well for one thing, he's a dipshit—he married my sister after all. And he's always caught bass—never fished for panfish." The officer shook his head and flicked his cigarette, then turned to face Clyde, including him in the story. "So the next morning he calls the DNR, and sure enough, the record for a bluegill in Michigan is eleven and a quarter. Dipshit goes in the trash and digs out the skin, puts it in a plastic bag, and tries to get a DNR officer to piece it together and measure it, but they won't do that. They just confirmed it was a bluegill. He's going to pay three hundred bucks to have a taxidermist build him a new fish from the scraps."

Clyde smiled. The only things he had with him were the clothes he wore and the ten-inch black-and-white television on his lap. "Wow," he said, "that's a big bluegill. I used to catch them about the size of my hand. I can't even imagine one twelve inches."

He wondered if the officers thought he was lying—he didn't look like a typical fisherman. He had twelve years' worth of hair tied in a ponytail and the anemic look of a man who doesn't go outside. But he had fished a lot as a boy: catfish, bass, bluegill, once for Wisconsin salmon. He didn't care what they thought.

The short one walked into the control center. The tall one stood there. "So you're taking your TV home with you, huh?"

"I wanted to bring something to remind me."

"Think you'll ever watch it?"

"I don't know. Maybe I'll retire it."

The officer looked up at the clear sky. "Nice day to go home. Don't come back. Too many of you do."

"I won't," Clyde said. "Thanks." He thought the officer might shake his hand, but he didn't. He walked into the control center too and Clyde watched the cigarette butt smoke and smolder on the sidewalk.

He'd gone to the classes, but nothing can prepare you. No one ever told him that a steak and shrimp dinner at Applebee's may nearly cause him to have an emotional breakdown, or that riding in a car would make him nervous and a little ill. No one told him he would want to hug everyone he met at the gas station on the way home, or that the smell of gasoline as he filled the tank would cause him to blink back tears. No one had told Clyde he might buy a seven-dollar bag of beef jerky with Melissa's money and cradle it in his arms like a baby.

Back in prerelease class, Miss Ruttinger had spoken about the traps that awaited them: mostly falling back in with old friends and the frustration that would come from trying to do the right thing, always with the label *ex-con* dogging their every step. It would be hard, she told them, which was why—no matter what she said or how they all felt then—more than half of them would return.

People from the outside came to the class to give pointers on everything from balancing a checkbook to conflict resolution. He went every Wednesday for three months and no one—not even the successful ex-inmate who called himself Duck—had told him that when he walked into his house he would hear again the tiny voices of his children, though they were grown, in college, and wouldn't be home to welcome him for two more days. No one told him he would be afraid to slide back the glass door to the patio and step into the yard. It seemed too open somehow.

Clyde stood at the glass door watching the dog he'd never met, barking, apparently, at the fence. She would run to the other end, wait a few seconds, then return to the spot where she'd barked. It was hopeful, how the dog desperately wanted something to be there to bark at, but even if there wasn't, she barked anyway. The dog did this over and over again until she suddenly took off at full speed around the yard twice, then began the routine again. He watched Melissa's reflection come up behind him. He could see the bright teeth of her smile, her shiny hair pulled back in a ponytail. She wore a bright black leather belt around a blue tie-dyed shirt that hung to the middle of her thighs. Under the shirt were red leggings. His life in prison had aged her—she had streaks of gray in her hair now and grooves fanning from the outside corners of her eyes—but she was still very pretty. She looked happy, healthy, and as lithe as a runner in marathon form. In the glass, she looked like the same girl he'd met twenty-one years ago. She wrapped her arms around his waist. "Her name's Margo," she said.

"She looks like a Margo. She's gorgeous." The dog was black and sleek, muscular, young, and energetic. She barked for a spell, ran a lap around the yard, then continued barking again. The dog had done this so many times it seemed to be her job. "What's she barking at?"

"Nothing," Melissa said. "That's where I shine the laser pointer at night—from the door and back again—to wear her out, otherwise she's up and down off the bed all night."

"What's a laser pointer?"

She squeezed his waist. "I love you, Clyde. Welcome home."

"I love you too," he said, and they watched the dog run, then bark, and run, then bark.

Melissa had always seemed to attract the strangest of strays. She named them whatever came to her mind during yoga, the same way she'd named all three of their children: Ocean, Azure, and Malachi. He loved the names because they belonged to his children, but where he was from, names were more traditional, less oddball and bohemian. Oddly, all the dogs she ever named had more reasonable, human names, always beginning with an *M* for some reason: Mitch, Missy, Misty, Michael—among the twenty or so he had once known.

It wasn't only dogs either. Neighborhood children, always looking slightly underfed and unwashed, gravitated toward her. She talked to them like valued citizens, gave them small jobs to do around the house, taught them how to draw colorful cat faces on paper plates, and loved them in her way. All of the stray animals and wandering kids had been nerve-racking to Clyde at times, and at times he'd been jealous of her endless supply of patience and love for others, but he had always returned to the obvious, essential question: how could you not love a woman like that?

Melissa held him there by the back glass door, watching the dog repeat her loop. "Would you like to see the womb?" she asked.

"The womb?"

"In the basement. Actually, *the* basement," she said proudly, smiling. "It's so perfect."

She had written something of the sort a while back, but he had forgotten the details. It was nearly impossible to keep track of all her projects, life changes, and new diets. She never followed through on many of them but apparently the basement project she'd stuck out.

"Sure," he said. They walked through the kitchen and he noticed one of her socks was dark gray and the other was blue. At the basement door Clyde lingered at the threshold, hand on the jamb. "I guess this here would be the vagina?"

"Wow, Clyde!" She studied the frame and the door itself, running her hands over the wood grain on the door. "And look at that—I never noticed it before, but the wood design is perfect."

"It was always my experience that the door would be closed and bolted shut."

She slapped his shoulder playfully and they walked down the stairs. He tried to think of another metaphor, something funny, but nothing came to mind. After twelve years around men, it didn't surprise him to be out of practice with flirty jokes.

Melissa flicked the basement light on. The overhead track lights cast a lavender glow that darkened the rough-spackled, velvety, and placental-pink painted walls. They were hung with four large oil paintings of psychedelic, electric-looking, large-hipped pregnant women. They were all painted with a fluorescent palette of purple, green, red, and yellow, using only curved and circular lines, radiating an energy outside their silhouettes. They were a shock to his drab, prison-accustomed eyes, and they made him dizzy.

"Well, what do you think about the paintings?" she said.

"They're pretty crazy."

"Get this, the artist used the freeze-dried placentas from her own children to paint the darker reds. Isn't this such a healing room? I love it. Let's just sit here a minute." She led him to the pink velour couch. Nearby, on a small table against the wall, there was a large white candle made from hundreds of little wax balls. "I think of that as the heart of the room," she said.

"It's a cool candle for sure," said Clyde. He walked over and pulled one of the little wax marbles from the glass container. Looking from the top, he could see a white wick winding its way down through the spaces between them. It had never been lit.

"Light it," she said. "I didn't realize this until just now, but I guess I've been saving it for you."

Even the lighter she handed him was dark red. He lit the candle, looked at his hand, and smiled. "A lighter," he said. "I thought I'd never see one of these again."

He had met Jesus not long after getting to prison. He was a drug trafficker from Mexico City with a wiry, birdlike build and a beatific portrait of a crucified Christ on his forearm. Every Tuesday Jesus and a few others would make some kind of candy in the dayroom microwave. Clyde never tasted it, as those who made it always split the finished product among themselves, but he had watched it being made perhaps one hundred times. Jesus seemed to be the head chef, combining the powdered milk, water, sugar, and hot sauce in a bowl, then microwaving the ingredients down into a syrupy, sticky goo. The room would stink of burned milk. Clyde figured that was how every cozy adobe in Mexico smelled.

After all of the ingredients had been microwaved, Jesus would carefully lift the hot bowl by its edges, set it on the table, and use two bright orange chow hall spoons to make the candies. He would scoop a perfectly proportioned glob of the sticky, white concoction and roll it into a ball using only the two spoons—flipping and rolling and squeezing, all the while chatting with his amigos in loud, rapid Spanish. The quick, smooth movements of molding the candy resembled frenzied knitting, yet with the finesse of a magician's sleight-of-hand trick.

When the candy was cooler, he'd drop it onto the inside of the bowl's lid, which held a thick layer of sugar. With his fingertips, Jesus coated the piece of candy, then set each one on the backside of one of the pink disbursement forms everyone used as scrap paper. The forming and rolling of each candy took twenty seconds, and each batch made over fifty marble-size pieces.

Clyde had never thought much about it until now, but he wanted to taste it more than anything. Back then, overcome by the smell of burned marshmallows and rancid cream, the thought of putting one of them in his mouth had repulsed him. But now he stood there watching the new candle burn and realized for the first time how much he had loved watching the family of Hispanic inmates, and how he would never see them again.

He had lied, Clyde thought. To the officer that morning when he said he would never return. He was back now, and he would return every day for the rest of his life.

"Did the candle hypnotize you?" Melissa asked.

"Yeah. I guess so." He dropped the wax ball next to the flame and sat down beside her on the couch.

"I think if we had had this room back then," she said, "you wouldn't have done it."

"I don't know."

"I would have made you sit down here for at least two hours every night and heal your issues. You had a lot of anger."

"I know."

"You've never thought about killing me, have you?"

"I never meant to kill anyone."

"I know," she said. "I just worry."

He kissed her on the cheek and hugged her. "Do you mind if I take a nap? It's been a long day."

She gave him a look he hadn't seen in twelve years: an intense yet distant stare, as if she was looking through him hoping to find someone she liked better. A slight, pressed-lip smile barely concealed a smoldering fire. He had worked long hours in car sales at a Chevy dealer in Kalamazoo, and on his Sundays and Mondays off he woke well before Melissa so he could work in the yard, smoking his menthol cigarettes in the dewy coolness of the morning. He weeded the flower beds and pulled the dead heads off the flowers, and when the dew burned off he picked up the dog crap and mowed. Later he would nap for a couple of peaceful afternoon hours, and this never failed to infuriate Melissa. When he'd see her again in the kitchen or living room, her body would ring like a bell with disgust. She wouldn't look him in the eye, could hardly be in his presence until a couple of hours had passed. It wasn't rational in the least, he thought, but what can you do?

"Just a little rest," he said.

"I thought we might have sex."

"If I did that right now, Melissa, I think my brain might explode. I'm used to sleeping a little after lunch. I just need to lie here for a while."

"I'm sorry you don't love me anymore," she said.

"What?"

"How do you think that makes me feel? I feel super-rejected right now."

"You can sit here and heal until I wake up."

She stood abruptly, put her hands on her hips, staring down at him. Clyde could feel her entire body debating whether or not to engage with the issue.

"Melissa," he said, but had nothing to follow the plea with. His stomach fluttered. He was out of his element here in her womb-room. It was as if he had never left. He had traveled instantly back in time twelve years. "Holy shit," he said, without knowing exactly what he meant.

"That's just great." She went over to the candle and

blew it out with an aggressive breath of air. "Don't waste my fucking candle." She turned off the row of lavender lights, then stomped up the stairs, slamming the door to the womb on her way out.

He awoke around three to the sound of the garage door closing. For a moment he thought it was a neighboring cell door sliding shut. The basement was windowless and completely dark, much darker than it had ever been in prison, where the hall lights were always on and the tall floodlights that lit the grounds outside shone through the small cell windows all night.

He lay on the couch and could hear Melissa come through the back door. Her car keys hit the counter and slid to the wall. He knew exactly where they were, just to the left of the kitchen sink. She let the dog in and Margo's nails clicked on the kitchen linoleum. "Who's a good girl? Who's a good, pretty girl, huh?" he heard, and the dog went berserk, racing from the living room and sliding across the kitchen floor. "Oh, boy, she's a happy girl. Did you bark at the fence while Mommy ran to work? Did you meet Daddy, or is he still asleep?"

Clyde smiled. He felt good. Maybe the basement really did heal.

The door at the top of the stairs opened and a muted shaft of light swept away the dark. Melissa came down and turned on the lavender lights. The dog stood at the top of the stairs, unwilling to make the descent.

"I really like this basement," Clyde said. "It's so dark. Do you mind if I hook my TV up down here?"

"No, I don't mind. Are you hungry?" She smiled at him. "How about pizza? Do you still like pizza?"

"Who stops liking pizza?"

Clyde was sitting upright. He stretched toward the ceiling. Melissa held out her hand, and he took it. She pulled him up from the couch, smiling at him, apparently no longer mad. "You feel like you weigh exactly the same as you always did. That's crazy, for twelve years. It's some kind of record, I bet."

"Thank you, I guess," he said, following her up the stairs, holding the hand she trailed behind her. She stopped at the door. "Are you ready to meet Margo?"

"Yeah," he said. "Then I'm going to surprise you with something. Do we have any milk?"

In the kitchen Clyde said hello to the dog, who barked twice then curled up with Melissa on the living room couch as she ordered a pizza for delivery. Every five minutes or so, the dog came into the kitchen to bark at Clyde, then went back to Melissa, who had begun taping a program on the Incas for her seventh-grade students. The documentary was called *The Trail to Machu Picchu*. It followed the husband-and-wife hosts and their supply-carrying donkeys, Cervantes and Donkey Hotey, around the ancient ruins of Cuzco, Peru.

"Where's the milk?" Clyde said.

"Where it always is. In the fridge."

"I'm looking there, but I don't see it."

"It's soy milk. It says *Silk.* Cow milk is horrible for you, not to mention how they mistreat the cows. Did you hear the names of these donkeys?"

"Yeah, pretty funny." After the milk, he found the sugar, which he realized was nonprocessed raw stuff that looked like tiny amber gems in his palm. He found a small container of ground cayenne pepper behind a tiny bottle of vanilla extract. He combined two cups of the soy milk, a half cup of sugar, and a full tablespoon of the pepper.

"It's a reference," said Melissa, "to the writer Cervantes and his most famous book."

"Yeah, I got it. Prison didn't make me stupid. I've actually read *Don Quixote.*" He hadn't actually read more than two hundred pages, and he immediately felt petty and guilty for lying.

The general library at E. C. Brooks had consisted of ten tall shelves behind the front desk. He'd had to write down possible books from the card catalog, hand the list to the inmate librarian, and wait patiently for him not to find them. The books were invariably missing, the card catalog horribly outdated. He'd gone along with the broken system until he'd gotten wise to the ways of prison, then bribed the librarian with a bag of coffee and was snuck among the musty-smelling stacks while the staff library head was in her office. Clyde's heart pounded like he was making a break for it, grabbing at Cervantes and other big classics that would last him a while, among them *Moby-Dick,* which he'd actually finished.

He'd never thought about Cervantes again, until now.

Clyde brought the mixture to a slow boil and walked into the living room. The male host of the show was speeding slightly from chewing coca leaves. He talked quickly and his movements were jerky and involuntary. As he sat atop his donkey speaking to the camera, he kept looking behind him and feeling his head to make sure his sombrero was still there. His partner was silent and Clyde wondered if she was angry about his high.

"This was used by the Incas to attract hummingbirds," said the host, pointing to a bright peach-colored flower with drooping, nectar-laden petals and long, brown and yellow stamens. "And down go the donkeys." The TV bleeped a curse word as Chuck hopped off his donkey, lying down in the center of the trail. "Now watch Donkey Hotey—he's a follower, and he'll do the same thing." His wife climbed off and, as if on cue, the second donkey lay down. "When they get tired," Chuck said, "there's no stopping them. They simply take a nap."

Clyde watched Melissa. Surely she saw the connection, the vindication. It was animal instinct, which was nothing to be argued with. She had always oohed and aahed over animals on TV: he wanted her to say something about the napping donkeys so he could really address the point. "Do you see the irony?" he would say. But Melissa would say nothing, just sit there watching stoically, her hand scratching the dog; he knew she would never give in and their relationship now was the same as when he'd left. He loved her for this, and knew that without her stubbornness she would not have such strength. It was her strength that had raised his children, kept the home, paid the bills, and stayed with him when he had fully expected her to go after the first couple of years. How could he not love her?

"Ugh," Melissa said. "What is that smell?"

"Oh shit!" He ran to the stove.

"Jesus, Clyde, it smells like something dead burning."

"That's how it smells," he said. "That's how it always smells."

The bottom of the pot had burned black but above it the sugar in the mixture had caramelized, reducing the mixture into a thick, slowly churning concoction, turning darker by the second. Clyde turned the flame off. He tried rolling the mud-colored taffy into balls using spoons but couldn't, so he rinsed Melissa's yellow dish gloves and rolled about twenty balls with gloved hands, coating them in the raw, brown, crystalline sugar. He laid them on a white, plastic plate for presentation. They looked like tiny Christmas ornaments coated with dangerous smoked glass.

The dog clicked into the kitchen and before Clyde thought better of it, he tossed one of the candies to her. She chewed it up, then gagged and forced most of it out of her mouth. She lapped up water from her bowl for nearly a minute. "You didn't give Margo one of those stinky sugar balls, did you?" Melissa called.

"No," he said, wiping up the mess with paper towels. He couldn't remember one instance of lying during his entire stint in prison. Now he had just lied twice in the past twenty minutes.

The doorbell rang and the pizza arrived. Melissa set the box on the dining room table next to Clyde's TV. He set the plate of candy on the counter, then picked up his television set. "What kind of pizza?" he asked.

"Oh, no. I got vegetarian without thinking. I guess I forgot you were here."

He looked down at Margo, who stuck close to the water bowl—even despite the pizza delivery person at the door. Clyde shook his head. "Did I ever leave?" he asked the dog.

He took his TV in one arm and picked a piece of candy off the plate. He walked down to the basement, lit the candle, and popped the candy into his mouth. He set the TV on the floor and hooked it up to the cable jack. The candy was sweet at first, then quickly turned a burned marshmallow bitter, which was bearable until the heat began, as if it was a candied jalapeño. It singed his tongue and caused his entire head to itch with a cold sweat. He turned on the television. The stations ran up to 100, showing nothing but static. He reconnected the jack, but nothing changed. He flipped the channels and the room flashed from static bright to a dim red darkness, like a crude strobe light. He turned off the TV, then spit out the hideous candy into the melting pool of wax balls.

For a moment he stood above the flame, feeling the pulse of light from the candle. Where was he? Physically, he knew—572 Lancelot Lane, just outside of Kalamazoo.

But he had to find a job. He had to get a driver's license and make contact with his parole officer. He was at the beginning again in the middle of his life, and all the good parts appeared to be over: the kids growing up, climbing the career ladder, family trips everyone would always remember. Creating those memories must be the "good" part of life, yet he'd spent all those golden years behind bars. He'd known it then; at night, waves of pain radiated out from the life he was missing, rocking him with gusts of intense sadness. And now, a similar pain belted him, as intense as the heat from the horrible candy.

He heard the dog whining at the top of the stairs. Wasn't it good to be here? Wasn't it good to be free? Clyde felt his face warm from the candle's flame.

He would love Melissa like he was supposed to. He would be a productive contributor to society again. He would get the cable fixed in the basement, teach the dog to descend the stairs, and spend many hours there with her as he healed. And once he had, once he was finished, he would do everything better than he ever had—after he felt more at home. When he felt like this was his basement, Melissa was his partner, Margo his dog, the yard and the house, all his. When this world felt like his again, he would begin.

ACKNOWLEDGMENTS

The night I killed a man was a horrible ordeal, especially for his family, my family—everyone traumatized by my actions. I still struggle with guilt and sorrow. There's often so much sadness and grief in my heart, it feels like I might explode. But you learn within twenty-four hours of hearing a prison door slam shut, either you will die regretting the past or you'll learn to live in the present. For me, fiction is a large part of that present, and I hold on to it like a lifeboat drifting daily from the fog.

Though this book may feel too thin to hold the weight of all these thanks, I'm not taking for granted that I will ever pass this way again, so:

A huge debt of gratitude goes to my sister, Nicole Browning, and her family: Bill, Tyler, and Morgan. Nicole, besides being a mother of teens and having a separate full-time job, has typed everything I've ever sent her. She does it cheerfully and without pay. Like an angel.

A special thanks to Jarrett Haley, who found three short stories of mine in Aaron Burch's *Hobart* eight years ago, and never stopped believing until that belief became a book, one he worked tirelessly on to improve. And to Jarrett's family—his wife, Nicolle, and the cutest kids you've ever seen: Oliver, Charlotte, and Priscilla. Also Jarrett's mother, Patricia Jordan, who typed in the countless changes and revisions.

Thank you to Elise Capron and Sandra Dijkstra at the Sandra Dijkstra Literary Agency. Your enthusiasm and fierce business prowess is a gift I wasn't expecting. Thank you!

I will be forever indebted to Kathryn Belden, fearless Scribner editor extraordinaire and friend, who took a chance on an inmate. And to Nan Graham and the rest of the good folks at Scribner who empowered her to take that chance.

To my sister, Shelley Eaton, and her family—Jim, Parker, and Grant—for all of their love and support.

To Don and Sherie Knutsen, Kris, Clint, and Lucy.

And to Warren and Arllis, my mom and dad. Anything good in these pages came from you. Thank you for all of your love and support!

It is impossible for me to describe the escape I feel when watching the Detroit Tigers for a few hours a day, 162 (and sometimes more) a year. Since 2006, when all we could buy were black-and-white TVs and the great

Jim Leyland managed, they have been like dependable friends—often maddening, but always there. I would be lost and a lesser person without them!

Thanks to all my teachers at Southern Illinois U and Western Michigan U, who taught me that words could change the world: Stuart Dybek, Jaimy Gordon, Elizabeth McCracken, Beth Lordan, Carolyn Alessio, Lucia Perillo, Rodney Jones, Ricardo Cortez Cruz, and the late Kent Haruf.

To Bridgett Jensen, my "oldest" friend and sender of many books. And to friends along the way: Shelly Barton, Trace Roberson, Andrea Nolen, and Darrin Doyle.

Thank you to the literary journals that stuck my stories in their pages and gave me hope: *Oyez Review, Dislocate, Bull, Hobart, Foliate Oak, Cooweescoowee, Trajectory, Iconoclast, Phantasmagoria, Beloit Fiction Journal,* and *Vice.* And to the hundreds of journals that didn't.

To the incredible Kim Knutsen: my best friend, my favorite writer and funniest PhD, and the world's best mother to the lights of my life, the reasons I'm still alive: Henry, Elijah, and Lily Rose. I would give anything to be there and not here.

Last but not least, to the too many prisoners in the United States, who are the inspiration for these stories. I pray that we all find forgiveness, freedom, and peace. Inside and out. And my avid-reading inmate friends so far: Myrle Wheat, Craig Haskell, Michael Fritz, Lou Longoria, and Garry Steffenhagen.

Every penny I might be fortunate enough to make as a result of my writing goes into an education fund for my kids.

From Convicted Murderer to Debut Author. Curtis Dawkins answers questions about his crimes, life on the inside, and his debut story collection, *The Graybar Hotel*

Countless authors have tried to capture what goes on inside a prisoner's mind, but how much do they really know?

Curtis Dawkins began drinking when he was twelve; later, alcohol turned into a big enough problem that he dropped out of college. He entered rehab, then Alcoholics Anonymous. He got sober and by the late '90s had earned an MFA in creative writing from Western Michigan University, married fellow writer Kimberly Knutsen, and started a family.

But as time progressed, Dawkins began taking prescription painkillers. His addiction grew to ketamine and heroin. On Halloween Night in 2004, he attempted to rob Thomas Bowman on the porch of his home in Kalamazoo, Michigan. When Bowman resisted, Dawkins—who was high on crack and had drank alcohol for the first time in years—shot him in the chest. He then proceeded inside, where he threatened Bowman's roommate. A SWAT team had arrived by then, and Dawkins held the roommate hostage. Three hours later, he walked out of his own volition and was taken into custody.

In July 2005, Dawkins was convicted of Bowman's murder and found guilty of eight other charges related to the incident and sentenced to life in prison with no possibility of parole. Inside, Dawkins began to write again. Eventually, he started submitting to literary journals, with his sister's help. An agent took notice and sold a collection of Dawkins's stories to Scribner. That collection, now titled *The Graybar Hotel,* takes readers beyond prison cells and reveals the idiosyncrasies, tedium, and desperation of long-term incarceration. The stories also go deep into the characters' pasts, exploring what their lives were like before prison and their lingering troubles. The result is a rich portrait of a frequently forgotten crossroads of humanity.

Adam Vitcavage, media critic, corresponded with Dawkins about prison life, the controversy swirling around his book, and how writing remains an integral part of his life.

Adam Vitcavage: I just want to start with the basics of this collection. When did you start writing the stories that eventually made it into *The Graybar Hotel*?

Curtis Dawkins: I began writing the first story in the collection, "County," literally hours after arriving at quarantine, the first stop of any posttrial prison sentence. It was as if my brain, relieved at being out of the cramped, overwhelming county jail after eleven months, wanted to revisit the place in order to wring some sense out of the experience. The first sentence of the story: "Italian Tom was a saucier until a Cadillac doing sixty hit him and knocked the recipes out of his head," kept repeating itself in my head, until I wrote it down. And then I figured, "I've got nothing else to do, I might as well keep going." Which is how most of the things I write get written.

AV: When you were writing these, was the goal always publication?

CD: At first, no. This was late in '05, and for the first time in my writing career, I wrote just for the sake of writing. Then ambition entered through the side door when my longtime partner and great novelist Kim Knutsen said she loved "County," which she thought I should call "Bob" (she still thinks it should be called that), and that I should send it out to see if I could get the story published. I couldn't.

But a huge side benefit in my renewed love of writing was that, for the first time in a year, I was not thinking of the horrible tragedy and disaster I had caused. Writing was a tremendous, and probably lifesaving, relief. It was, and is, hugely therapeutic, just in the sense that writing gets my mind off reality.

AV: These stories are very humanizing, which I think is important. How did you create such vibrant, nuanced characters?

CD: These are the people I know. They are all amalgams of the men I've spent more than a decade with. I'm thrilled that you found the stories humanizing, which is more the reality than the cliché muscle-bound, tattooed, shank-wielding subject of screens both large and small. Those men are in every prison, of course, but I am interested in what is underneath. That shank wielder might be great at origami or have a daughter he adores. I guarantee you there is something about him that is unique and possibly beautiful. All I do is pay attention, maybe fill in some unknowns with details of my own imagining.

AV: "573543" really stood out to me. It touches on the theme of addiction. Was a lot of this drawn from personal experience, or did you stray from making this with a lot of biographical elements?

CD: "573543" might be the most biographical, until the very last story, where the inmate goes home, becomes true.

The titular number is my actual prison number, and the drug abuse, while no excuse for anything, has been a fact of my life since the age of fifteen or sixteen. It is a fact of nearly every inmate's life. Though so is softball and rain, rooting for the Tigers, and people who disappear. And jackasses gleefully chirping that your season is over.

I was having fun experimenting with fiction disguised as nonfiction, as well as the creepy fact that a dead man's number is often reissued.

AV: I always ask every author this: What do your daily writing schedule and habits look like?

CD: I write every day except Sunday. I start at about 11 a.m., until we go to lunch between 12 and 1. Then I print out (my typewriter has memory, so it works like a word processor) what I've worked on, and work on improving it. Or scrapping it and starting anew.

I have found that writing for more than a couple of hours per day really doesn't accomplish anything. I try to stop when I know what is going to happen next. That seems to prime the pump for the next day. I think most of my writing is done in my mind without my help after the actual physical writing is finished.

And I'm always reading fiction. Always looking for new writers, and old writers I've never heard of, to read. The first job of writers is to read.

AV: What does writing mean for your life?

CD: Most of the guys in prison have no purpose to their life. A person needs that, something to work at, goals to pursue. Writing gives me that. No matter how hard it is, I'm grateful, and I never take it for granted.

AV: When I told people I'd be sending you some questions, and explained your background, I got a lot of mixed responses. Is how people perceive you and this book something you think or care about at all?

CD: I have mixed responses about myself every day, so I don't blame people who know me only by a list of facts to feel similarly. I would feel the same about any inmate if I were in their shoes.

I would urge those suffering from “mixed” feelings to read the stories. If they still feel that way, write me a letter.